Once Upon a Cruise

ONCE UPON a CRUISE

Anna Staniszewski

SCHOLASTIC INC.

ISBN 978-0-545-87986-6

10 9 8 7 6 5 4 3 2 1   16 17 18 19 20

Printed in the U.S.A.   40
First printing 2016

Book design by Yaffa Jaskoll

"Anyone can hold the helm
when the sea is calm."
-Publilius Syrus

Chapter 1

I still can't believe we're on a Disney cruise!" a tiny blond girl beside me squeals.

I close my eyes and repeat the Fairy Tale Cruises employee motto in my head: *Be helpful, friendly, and fun!* That means no correcting the passengers, even if this is the thirteenth person so far today who's been totally wrong. Instead, I force myself to smile and focus on offering passersby squirts of hand sanitizer as they head into the dining hall for dinner. We only left port a couple hours ago and already my face hurts from smiling. After a whole summer of this, my cheek muscles will be so strong, I'll probably be able to lift weights with them.

Then the blond girl gasps. "Look, there's Cinderella!"

"Wow!" her dark-haired friend says. "But why is her dress the wrong color? And why isn't she wearing glass slippers? Are you sure that's even Cinderella?"

I can't take it anymore. "Actually," I butt in, "it's Aschenputtel."

The girls stare at me. They're probably about six years old and dressed in sparkly pink from head to toe, like mini Barbies.

"What's an *ash puddle*?" the blond girl asks, raising an eyebrow at me.

"That character over there isn't Cinderella," I explain in my most cheerful voice. "It's Aschenputtel from the Grimm brothers' fairy tale. It's a lot like Cinderella's story, but instead of a fairy godmother, there's a tree that grants wishes." Well, my literature professor dad would be proud of me, but judging by the skeptical looks on the girls' faces, they are *not* impressed.

Technically, Disney doesn't own the rights to Cinderella's character, but Fairy Tale Cruises isn't taking any chances or they might get sued, which is why they're using characters that most people haven't heard of. At least that's the impression I got from slogging through the million-page-long manual my mom gave me after she took a last-minute job as the ship's cruise director.

"So she's not Cinderella?" the blond girl asks.

"She's . . . sort of like Cinderella's cousin," I say, but the mini Barbies aren't listening to me anymore.

"Look! It's Rapunzel!" the one with dark hair cries. She grabs her friend's hand, and they rush off toward a young woman dressed as Petrosinella, aka the Italian version of Rapunzel.

"I can't believe that weird girl didn't even know who Cinderella is," I hear the blonde say before they both disappear into the mob of passengers.

It's so hot and humid out that I'm pretty sure my eyeballs are sweating. I try to casually mop my cheek with my polyester sleeve before I go back to disinfecting people and chirping, "Remember, clean hands equal clean health!"

I should have known better than to correct the Barbie twins. They'll find out soon enough that none of the characters on the ship are from stories they know. But if one of the Spies heard me, I would have been in trouble.

"Ainsley!" I hear someone call.

I turn to find my new bunkmate, Katy, shuffling toward me. Her legs are bound together so tightly that she can barely move, but her sparkly mermaid costume is glowing in the sun, making her look like some kind of seaweed goddess. My fingers itch to grab the small camera I always keep tucked in my pocket and take her picture, but things like that are Not Allowed while we're on duty.

"Thank goodness I found you," she says. "I needed to see a friendly face."

"What happened?"

"Some little kid pinched me!" She lets out a high-pitched giggle.

"Ouch!" I say with a sympathetic cringe.

"I was just posing for pictures by the main staircase," she chatters on, "talking to what I thought was a nice family, and suddenly—bam! Right on my behind!" Funny how she's sixteen, more than three years older than I am, but she's still embarrassed to say words like *butt*. "Oh, I forgot to tell you. A few of the other sea creatures might go hang out at the Oven tomorrow night."

"The Oven?"

She rolls her eyes. "Terrible name, right? It's supposed to be the ship's teen lounge and nightclub. You want to come?"

"I can't," I automatically say. Then I remember that the whole point of taking this job was for me to not have to constantly watch over Mom anymore. "Wait, maybe I can come. What time?"

"Whenever they let us off our shifts," Katy says. "I never thought being a mermaid would be so exhausting! You're so lucky you're in the show, Ainsley. Then you know exactly when you're done for the night. Plus, you get to actually *be* the character instead of just prancing around in a silly costume!"

Katy's voice is loud and brassy, not exactly how you'd expect the Mermaid Princess (as she's called here) to sound. I can see people shooting her confused looks as they walk by. Then again, maybe it's because she's dressed more like a fish with long hair than Ariel from the Disney movie.

Suddenly, I spot one of the Spies nearby, dressed in his crisp, white uniform. Uh-oh. He's looking right at us. My stomach dips, and it's not just from the movement of the ship.

Mom claims the "monitors" are only on the ship to make sure everything runs smoothly the first few days and that no one does anything that will get us sued, but I bet they scurry to the captain the minute we do something wrong.

"Um, we should probably talk about this later." I try to give Katy a meaningful look, but she's on a roll. She's one of the sweetest people I've ever met, but she's also a serious talker. Last night, our first night aboard the ship, she kept me awake for hours, telling me all about her dog, Snoopy, who's back home with her parents in Tennessee.

"I did try out to be in the show," she goes on, "but they said the only spots left were—"

"Remember to remain in character at all times," the Spy hisses at us.

Katy jumps like she's just heard a snake. Clearly, she didn't notice him lurking until now. I glance at his name tag and shake my head. Of course his name is Curt. It matches his personality perfectly.

"Sorry," Katy whispers. Then her eyes widen and she chirps, "Soooorry!" in her Mermaid Princess voice. She gives me a panicked look and starts waddling toward the pool.

"You're Ainsley Parker, right?" Curt asks, turning to me.

I swallow. Is he asking my name so he can report me? I can't get in trouble on the first day and risk making my mom look bad!

"Um, yeah," I say. "I was just—"

7

"Shouldn't you be at the Once Upon a Time Theater right now?"

I grab today's schedule from my back pocket. Sure enough, I was supposed to report for rehearsal five minutes ago.

"Oops, sorry about that," I say, wondering how he knows my schedule better than I do. I mean, there are hundreds of crew members aboard this ship! "I guess time really flies when you're dousing people with hand sanitizer!"

Curt doesn't crack a smile. "Your replacement is on her way, so I'll take over from here," he says.

I gladly transfer my hand-spraying duties over to him and head to the theater on Deck 4. Tonight is the opening show, so we're supposed to do a final run-through this afternoon to make sure everything looks right. Mom has been going on and on about how the Fairy Tale Extravaganza will set the tone for the rest of the weeklong cruise. Hopefully, that means it'll go well. The last thing we want is for Fairy Tale Cruises' maiden voyage to start off on a bad note.

I weave my way through the throngs of people and head down a corridor that's blocked off with red tape so passengers won't use it. This is the last part of the ship to be repainted. All the refurbishing was supposed to be finished before we left Fort Lauderdale, but I guess things got behind schedule. Still, the ship looks amazing now compared to how it was a few days ago when Mom and I first saw it. Before Fairy Tale Cruises bought this ship, it was used as a knitting cruise. Seriously. Not only were there rocking chairs installed all over the ship for people to sit in and knit, but the entire bow was painted to look like a wool hat, and the rest of the ship was covered in knitting-themed murals.

The biggest of the murals—showing famous knitters throughout history all connected with strands of yarn—is the one that's being painted over right now. As I pause to admire the way the sunlight hits the faces of the people in the knitting web, one of them catches my eye. He looks familiar, but I can't figure out why. I glance around to make sure no one is watching before pulling my camera out of my pocket and snapping a picture. Then I hurry off to rehearsal before my mom starts to think I fell overboard or something.

When I get to the theater, the lights are all on and the stage is covered with people milling around. It takes me a minute to find my mom in the chaos. Finally, I spot her perfectly styled black bob at the far end of the stage. It's still kind of a shock to see her looking so put-together considering she was a wild-haired pajama dweller only a couple weeks ago, before she got this job offer. But that means Mom's "fresh start at sea" plan is actually working. Not only is she back to her old self, but I might even get to have a little fun this summer.

Mom's talking to the assistant cruise director, Aussie Andy, who's furiously scribbling down every-thing she says. Funny how before I was born, Mom used to be the one doing his job, and now here she is, in charge of the entertainment on the entire cruise. You'd never know it by the calm, collected look on her face, but I can tell she's nervous. The way her nose keeps twitching ever-so-slightly is a dead giveaway.

"All right, everyone!" Mom calls, clapping her hands. No one seems to notice. "Gather round!" she tries again, louder this time. Still no luck. Her nose twitches a tiny bit more. She's clearly a little rusty at all this.

Finally, a guy in a prince costume lets out a loud whistle that nearly shatters my eardrums. "Listen up!" he bellows.

Mom gives him a grateful smile, though everyone else looks a little annoyed. "Now, " she says, "we have an hour to run through the opening show one more time, so let's make it count, okay? Remember that I'll start things off with a welcome speech before the dwarves dance out onto the stage." Her eyes lock with mine through the crowd. "Oh! And we have our special guest, Briar Rose, here with us today. Everyone, say hello to my daughter, Ainsley!"

Everyone turns to look at me, and I feel my cheeks

growing hot. "Hey," I say, waving. "Um, I'm excited to nap onstage while you guys do all the work."

A couple of people chuckle while a few others seem to be sizing me up. I probably look like a little kid to them since I'm still a few weeks away from my thirteenth birthday. Briar Rose, the German version of Sleeping Beauty, was supposed to be played by a girl from Canada (and she was also going to be Katy's roommate), but she had to drop out at the last minute. Mom had just accepted the job as cruise director when it happened, and she thought having me take the girl's spot was the perfect solution. Even though I have no business being near a stage, in exchange for taking the part, I also got to take the girl's bunk instead of rooming with Mom. Considering my mom's extreme snoring, the offer was too good to turn down. Besides, battling stage fright is still better than staying with Dad for the summer.

While the other cast members shuffle into the wings to their places, I head into the audience to wait for my mom to be done.

And that's when I spot him.

He's wearing pointy shoes and green tights and elf ears, but he's still the cutest boy I've ever laid eyes on. He seems to be one of the dwarves, although I don't know which one. Bashful? Doc?

Wait, no. What am I saying? Those are Disney characters. I glance around, checking for Spies, paranoid that they might have heard my thoughts. Luckily, the coast is clear.

The dwarves line up behind Schneewittchen, which I guess is how you say Snow White in German. (Fairy Tale Cruises *really* isn't taking any chances with this whole getting sued thing.) Cute Dwarf stands sixth among the other dwarves, looking off into the wings as if he's contemplating something really deep. As my mom goes through her speech, he pulls a Moleskine notebook out of his pocket and jots something down.

Oh my gosh. Maybe he's a songwriter! There is nothing cuter than an artsy guy, and at my jock-filled junior high back home, there is a serious artist shortage. Finally, someone I might be able to talk to.

As if he can sense me staring at him, Cute Dwarf glances out at the audience and his eyes meet mine. I swear I feel the ground—or sea—move under me. And then he . . . well, he doesn't quite smile, but he gives me a soulful look, as if we share some kind of secret.

My entire body suddenly feels as if it's been plugged into an electrical socket. Cute Dwarf noticed me! He almost smiled at me!

Maybe this summer will be better than I thought.

Chapter 2

Mom comes into the audience after her part is over, while the dwarves start prancing around the stage. I can't help noticing that Cute Dwarf's prancing is just a touch more graceful than everyone else's.

Mom gives me a smile from the aisle and waves me toward the back of the theater.

"I was worried you weren't coming, Ains," she says softly when we're far enough away from the rehearsal.

"Sorry. I lost track of time. But you don't really need me here, do you?" As Briar Rose, my job—starting tomorrow evening—is to lie onstage every night and pretend to be asleep. Then, on the final night of the cruise, I'll finally wake up, yawn, stretch, and wave at the audience. That's it. The role was supposed to be bigger, back when the girl from Canada still had my part, but Mom did some last-minute cutting to avoid having me act in public. Considering my disastrous stage debut in second grade, we both decided that was for the best. Hopefully, I can at least handle sleeping onstage.

Mom shrugs. "I thought we should have you here today so you can get to know everyone. You'll be over there tomorrow." She points to a mattress in the corner of the stage, but when I ask her if I should go lie down on it for practice—maybe I can make up some of the sleep I missed thanks to Katy's late-night chatter—she shakes her head. "Actually, I was hoping you could do me a favor."

I swallow. Another favor? On top of spending my whole summer on a giant, crowded boat, away from all my friends? On top of giving up the big wildlife photography project I've been planning forever, so I can spray people with hand sanitizer and smile all day long and play a mannequin onstage despite my crippling stage fright?

But of course I can't say any of that because I'm Mom's "little trooper." She's always saying that my strength has kept her going ever since she and Dad got divorced. Besides, this temporary cruise director job is the first thing Mom has been excited about in months. When she got the call about it a couple weeks ago, she'd actually danced around the house in her pajamas! I had to go along with it, even if it meant giving up my summer, and now that I'm here, I'm determined to do whatever it takes to make it work.

"Sure. What do you need?" I say, flashing the fake smile again. It's starting to feel like my trademark.

"There's a towel-folding class that's scheduled every morning, and the woman who was supposed to lead it burned her finger on an iron today. So I was thinking you could take over."

"Me? But I don't know anything about towel folding! I've heard about the stuff they do here—swans and witches and peacocks. How am I supposed to teach anyone that?"

"We have a book in the library that will show you everything you need to know, and you can start with something simple. This is a class for young children, after all. If you do this for me, I'll switch you out of spray-bottle duty."

I sigh. She's got me there. I thought being one of the hand-sanitizer girls would be easy, but I had no idea that the job would be so mind-numbingly boring. I hope my other job at the dining hall will be better. "Okay, fine. I'll do it. As long as the kids don't mind learning how to fold towels into flat rectangles."

"Thank you!" Mom says, giving me her most gleaming smile. "You should probably go study up before dinner duty. I left a book all about towel folding on your bed."

Funny how she already put the book in my cabin. I guess she knows me too well.

"So, what do you think of the show?" she asks, glancing back at the stage.

A group of oversized toads are shimmying across the stage, or maybe they're dragons? The costumes are hard to tell apart, and I have no idea what the plot of the show actually is. Stefan, the show's director, doesn't seem to care too much about what's happening onstage. He's too busy flirting with one of the fairies in the wings. I make a mental note to snap a picture of Stefan's cheek for my friend Alyssa back home. She's got a weird collection of photographs of scars and moles and stuff that she's been putting together for years.

"The show's, um, good," I say. Normally, shows on cruise ships take years to put together and months to rehearse, but this one has only been in production for a few weeks. I guess considering that, it's not bad.

My eyes scan the room for Cute Dwarf again, almost as if they have a mind of their own. Finally, I spot him in the front row, hunched over his notebook, chewing on the end of his pen. Could he be any cuter?

Mom must see me staring because she whispers, "His name is Smith."

I snap my gaze away. "Um, what?"

"Prince Handsome up there? His name is Smith."

"Is that his first name or his last name?" Somehow, Cute Dwarf doesn't look like a Smith, but then again, I don't actually know anything about him.

"I have no idea, but all the girls have been fawning over him. That's why we cast him as the prince."

Wait, what?

I realize Mom's looking up at the stage at a guy in tights and shiny shoes with a halo of perfectly gelled curls around his head. I'm pretty sure he's the one who let out the annoyingly loud whistle earlier to get everyone's attention.

"Ew, him?" I blurt out. Smith has got to be the most generically good-looking guy I've ever seen, like something out of a Disney movie. I bet the cruise line could get sued just for having him on board!

Guys like Smith are so not my type. Perfection might be good for animated films, but when it comes to photography, flaws are what make people interesting and beautiful. Like Cute Dwarf's slightly crooked ears and his green eyes that are half-squinted at his notebook as if he might need glasses.

Mom laughs. "Sorry, Ains. I know it's weird to talk to your mom about boys." She glances at her watch. "Oops! I have to go meet with the captain."

"You mean with *Captain Hook*?" I say in a loud whisper.

"Shh! I told you not to call him that!" she scolds, but she's laughing as she rushes away.

I go back to watching Cute Dwarf out of the corner of my eye. Maybe if I'm really sneaky, I can get a picture of him.

After pulling my camera out of my pocket, I try to casually stroll along and get a clear shot of his face at the same time. That's why I don't notice the giant monster in my way until I smash right into it.

Crash!

My camera clatters to the floor as dozens of index cards shoot out of the beast's claws and fall all around us.

"Hey!" the monster roars.

"Ah!" I cry, jumping back as its red eyes glare down at me.

Everyone in the theater, including the people onstage, turns to stare at me. It's only when I manage to stop having a heart attack that I realize the ferocious monster looks more like a grinning boar. In fact, it's some guy in a hairy pig costume with a script under his arm.

The guy pulls off his furry pig head. He looks barely older than me, but he's scowling at me as if I'm an annoying toddler. "Do you mind? I'm trying to concentrate here."

"Sorry," I say as the performers start up again. I snatch my camera off the floor and shove it into my pocket, praying it didn't get scratched. Then I scramble to gather up some of the index cards. They're covered in surprisingly neat handwriting on both sides.

"It took me forever to write out all my lines," the guy grumbles as he snatches the cards off the floor. "Do you know how long it'll take to put these in order again?"

"I could help you," I offer.

He shoots me another cold look. "I think you've done enough already."

"S-sorry," I say again. "I was distracted by . . . something."

"Or by *someone*?" he says, smirking.

Did he notice me staring at Cute Dwarf? Was I really that obvious? I try to make a getaway, but the guy grabs my shoulder with a furry claw.

"Wait, you're Lydia's daughter, right?" he says.

"Yeah, I'm Ainsley." Will he go roar at Mom next?

"Ian," the guy barks at me.

"What are you?" I can't help asking, motioning toward his hideous costume.

He rolls his eyes. "I was supposed to play Prince Handsome, but then some higher-up at the cruise line put in a call, and suddenly his nephew, Smith Charming, waltzes in and takes over. So now I'm playing the Pig King."

"What's the Pig King?"

"Exactly! Why can't they just call me the Beast?" He glances up at the stage and sighs. "This show is going to be a disaster if Smith's the lead. Do you think he even realizes he has arms?"

I follow his gaze to where Smith is moving around the stage like a stiff marionette. The Pig King is right, but after he yelled at me, I suddenly feel myself siding with Smith. Okay, he's not all that graceful—nothing like Cute Dwarf—but thanks to his chiseled features, he certainly looks the part. How rude of Ian to flat-out say Smith's not good for the part.

"I think you make a fine pig," I tell him flatly, and then I push past him toward the door. I take one last look back, hoping to catch Cute Dwarf's eye one more time, but he and his dwarf posse are gone.

Chapter 3

When I get to my cabin—or "stateroom" as the passengers call it—I spot the towel-folding book on my bed right away. It's hard to miss since it's bigger than my pillow. How am I supposed to learn all this stuff overnight?

I have to practically shimmy over to the bunk beds since the cabin is so small. I'm pretty sure my closet at home is bigger than this entire room, and at least that's all mine. Here I have to step over piles of Katy's dangerously high heels and limbo under the millions of filmy scarves she hung around the room "for atmosphere." If the scarves all fall down at once, I'm pretty sure we'll drown in fabric.

This sharing-my-personal-space thing is kind of hard to get used to. At least I got the top bunk since Katy's afraid of heights, so when I pull the curtain closed around it, I have one tiny scarf-free oasis to myself.

After I grab one of the towels from the bathroom, I climb up to my bunk cocoon. I leaf through the towel-folding book until I find instructions on how to make a snake. That should be easy, shouldn't it? I get to work, but after fifteen minutes of intense concentration, I've only succeeded in making something that looks like a rolled-up towel. Great.

Disgusted, I take out my camera and start flipping through the most recent pictures. Sadly, the latest one is nothing but a blurry image of the floor. If only I hadn't smacked into Ian the Pig, I could be gazing at a picture of Cute Dwarf right now!

I wish more than anything that I could pick up the phone and call my best friends, Alyssa and Brooke. I can imagine Brooke taking one look at Cute Dwarf and making some kind of inappropriate animal sound.

One time when we saw a hot guy at the mall, she started howling at him like a monkey. Alyssa and I couldn't stop laughing at the terrified look on the guy's face as he ran the other way.

Even if the ship's phone and internet access weren't super expensive, it wouldn't do any good to try to contact my two best friends since they're both away at camp for the summer. I'll have to take as many pictures as possible so I'll be able to tell them all about my summer when I get home. Plus, remember to take pictures of interesting moles and scars for the weird collection that Alyssa's had going since we were in fifth grade. I think having two plastic surgeon parents has kind of messed with her brain.

Taking pictures of passengers is technically Not Okay according to the employee handbook, but Alyssa made me promise I'd do it. "You'll get to see thousands of people in their bathing suits this summer. It's like my dream come true!" she said the day before I left. Then she made her eyes all round and puppyish, and I couldn't say no. Besides, I doubt it counts as breaking the rules if I'm only taking a picture of a mole on someone's elbow.

I keep scrolling through my pictures and pause at the shot of the mural. The man in it stares back at me with a knowing smile as he loops yarn around his hand. I still can't put my finger on why he looks familiar, so I keep scrolling back through my pictures—Mom and me when we first got on the ship; Brooke and Alyssa midair at a trampoline park, celebrating the last day of school; me posing next to one of my framed photos at the town library—until I get to the ones that I know I shouldn't look at because they make me upset. They're of Dad and me at one of his poetry readings about six months ago. The now-familiar anger starts pulsing through me as I look at his smiling, bearded face, his arm wrapped around me as if everything is perfect. Even though only a few weeks later, he and Mom split up.

Ugh. I really hope Cute Dwarf is *not* a poet.

I shut the camera off and stuff it back in my pocket. The truth is, I'm not mad at Dad for leaving. I'm mad at him for not caring. Back when he and Mom were still together and fighting all the time, he'd tell me that everything was "just fine," even though he was spending less and less time at home. And then one day Mom asked him if he wanted to move out, and he left the very next day—without even trying to make things right. Mom cried for weeks afterward, and I even heard her calling Dad and begging him to come home, but he didn't. Instead, he got an apartment close to the university where he teaches and only came to see me on his designated days. And every time I tried to ask him about Mom, he would say it "wasn't logical" for them to be together. Come on! Only a robot talks like that!

At the end of the school year, Dad tried to convince me to come live with him for the summer, saying he didn't get to spend any time with me anymore. He even sent me a letter—written on stationery!—but I didn't read the whole thing. Instead, I flat-out told him no. Not only was he going to be busy working on his next book of poems the whole time, but I was still mad at him for leaving us as if he was checking out of a hotel room. So when Mom got the cruise ship job, it was actually nice to have an excuse to go with her, even if I didn't really want to be away all summer. And the fact that I'll finally have money at the end of the summer to buy a real, professional camera doesn't hurt either.

With a sigh, I pick up the towel-folding book again and start working on the snake. After a few more tries, I end up with something that looks sort of like a worm. It'll have to do. After all, how impressive do towel sculptures for little kids have to be?

I glance at my watch and realize it's time to get ready for my shift at the Lost Children Dining Room. I think they were going for a Hansel and Gretel thing, but just like a lot of other places on this ship, its name is kind of terrible.

After wrestling my food-serving uniform out of my miniscule closet, I pull my hair back and give myself a quick glance in the pea-sized mirror in the bathroom to make sure I look okay, just in case any cute dwarves happen to cross my path. For a second, I eye Katy's makeup bag before remembering the time I tried putting on Mom's super-waterproof mascara last year and had to go to school looking like a drowned raccoon because we didn't have any industrial strength makeup remover in the house. No, thanks.

Since I still have a little time before I have to go help serve dinner, I grab my camera and head out to the walking track on Deck 4, just outside the theater. Maybe if I'm lucky, I'll spot some fish swimming alongside the ship. It's not as exciting as photographing a squirrel nest, complete with baby squirrels, like I'd been planning to do over the summer before Mom took the cruise director job, but it's something.

Things around me are eerily quiet. Every other deck is crammed full of people, but the strong smell of fresh paint is probably keeping them away from this spot. I lean over the railing for a minute and breathe in the sea air instead. When we were still docked at Fort Lauderdale, there was a distinctly fishy stench, but now the air is fresh and clean and salty. It reminds me of home since our house isn't that far from the ocean.

Along the horizon, I spot a couple of birds flying in front of the clouds. That means we're still pretty close to land, even if we can't see it. I raise my camera, ready to snap a few pictures, when one of the doors behind me slams open.

"You can't be serious!" I hear a female voice saying in a posh British accent. "There is no textual evidence to suggest the prince would ever act that way!"

I turn to see Snow White, um, I mean, Schneewittchen, standing face to face with none other than Smith Charming.

"Of course he would," Smith says. "He's the hottest guy around. If the princess wasn't interested, he'd go somewhere else. That's why when you wake up, you should gasp when you see how hot I am so the audience will know for sure that you're into me. Maybe you could even faint a little."

Schneewittchen shakes her head. "The director didn't say anything about that. And besides, how will anyone in the audience know that I've fainted if none of the lines indicate it?"

Smith grins. "Oh, people will get it. Girls faint around me all the time. I have that effect on them." Just then, he catches me staring at him, and his grin widens. "See? This little girl can't take her eyes off of me."

"Um, excuse me? I'm thirteen," I can't help saying. Okay, not yet, but Smith can't be older than sixteen himself. "And this 'little girl' is going to be up onstage with you in the show."

He gives me a blank look. Clearly, he doesn't remember me from rehearsal.

"I'm playing Briar Rose," I explain.

His face lights up. "My apologies, my lady," he says, dipping into a stiff bow. "I didn't recognize you. Maybe you can settle this debate for us. Do you think Snow White would faint at the sight of me?"

"She's not called Snow White, remember?" I say, instinctively checking for nearby Spies. "And no, I doubt it. She just woke up from a coma. I don't think the first thing she'd do is pass out again. After all that time being almost dead, she's probably thinking about finding a bathroom."

Schneewittchen gives me a triumphant smile and sticks her hand out to me. "I'm Gemma. And yes, I'm from England." Clearly, she gets asked that question all the time. "You're Lydia's daughter, right?"

"Yes, I'm Ainsley. It's nice to meet you," I say, feeling as if I should be more formal around Gemma since she sounds so smart. "What are you reading?" The textbook tucked under her arm looks like something out of my dad's library.

"Vladimir Propp's *Morphology of the Folktale*. It's for my dissertation. I'm about to start my PhD in Russian folklore in the fall."

"You should talk to my dad. He's a literature professor. But he's more into poetry than folktales." Only after I say it do I remember that I'm not actually speaking to my dad these days.

"Ooh, I love professors!" Gemma coos. "I can't wait to be one. I thought this job would be good real-world experience, but so far . . ." She lowers her voice. "Honestly, I'm wondering why I'm even here."

"To meet me, of course," Smith says. He waggles his eyebrows at Gemma in a way that looks straight out of a cartoon. Does he seriously think things like that work on girls, especially ones who are older than him and clearly much smarter? Maybe I should channel Brooke and start making monkey sounds at him to scare him off.

Gemma only rolls her eyes and says, "It was nice to meet you, Ainsley." Then she hugs her book to her chest and heads off.

Meanwhile, Smith seems to lose all interest in her and turns back to me. "So, where are you from, Ashley?"

"Ainsley," I correct. I'm about to make a run for it, but then I remember what Ian the Pig said about Smith being some important person's nephew. Maybe I should play nice, just in case word gets back to the cruise line's higher-ups about Lydia's unfriendly daughter. Mom is stressed enough about things going perfectly on this cruise without having to worry about me not getting along with people. "I'm from Rhode Island. How about you?"

His face lights up, as if he's been waiting for someone to ask him that question. Then he launches into a whole spiel about how he's not really from one place because he's moved around from one exotic location to the next his whole life. The way he tells it, he practically grew up on luxury yachts. I can't tell if he wants me to be impressed or to pity his "unstable childhood." Mostly, I try not to fall asleep as he goes on and on.

I glance at my watch and realize that I only have a couple minutes to get to the Lost Children Dining Room, but when I interrupt Smith to tell him that, he says, "I'll walk you down there," and then keeps babbling. He jumps from surfing to weightlifting to hot dog eating, but all the topics have one thing in common: They're all about him. Snore.

Weirdly, as we walk around the ship, pretty much all the women we pass (and some of the guys too) stare at Smith as if he's a god. Ugh. If they could talk to him for a second, I'm pretty sure they'd immediately get over his good looks.

I spot Cute Dwarf coming around the corner when we get to Deck 3. He's out of his costume and looking amazing in skinny jeans and a faded T-shirt for a band I've never heard of. He flashes me a small smile and then seems to notice that I'm being escorted by Smith. His smile fades, and he ducks into a stairwell. No!

I want to run after him, but that wouldn't exactly be subtle. Plus, I have to report for work.

"Well, I have to go," I say, cutting Smith off mid-sentence. "See you around."

"It was nice talking to you, Ashley."

"It was nice being talked at," I can't help saying. He just gives me a big smile as I hurry away.

After I help a little girl who's wandering around looking for her parents—she came to the Lost Children Dining Room thinking kids should report there if they're separated from their families—I get into serving position behind the food counter. I've never been so relieved to put on a hairnet and apron. Anything is better than having to listen to Smith drone on and on about himself. But just as I dish out my first piece of chicken, Katy comes rushing over as fast as she can in her ridiculous mermaid costume.

"Ainsley," she says, panting, "your mom is looking for you. There's some kind of laundry emergency."

Laundry?

I stare at her for a second, sure I've heard wrong. Even if there is an emergency with laundry, why on earth would my mom want my help with it? But when I don't answer, Katy grabs my arm and says, "Quick, Ainsley. She needs a huge favor!"

Before I know it, she's yanking off my apron and pushing me toward the door. And then I'm off to do a favor for my mom. Again.

Chapter 4

As Katy and I rush toward the laundry area on the bottom deck, I try—and fail—to pull off my hairnet. Even though I've only been wearing it for a few minutes, it seems to have fused to my ponytail. I eventually give up and leave it flopping around on my head.

"Your mom was so panicked," Katy says. "She kept asking everyone where you were. Finally, she remembered you were on dinner duty, so she asked me to find you."

"But why? What happened?"

"I don't know, but she said you were the only one who could help her." Katy gives me a puzzled look as we dash into an elevator, and my stomach flops as we plunge down toward the laundry room. "Are you some kind of laundry genius?"

"What? No!" Granted, I do all the laundry at home these days. It used to be Dad's job since Mom refuses to go into our spider-infested basement. Now that he's gone, I'm the one who gets to dash in and out of the cellar while imagining little spider babies nesting in my ears.

"It's so sweet how much your mom depends on you," Katy says. "Like yesterday when she asked you to double-check all her notes for the show. I wish my parents trusted me like that. They're still mad at me for blowing off summer college prep classes to go work on a cruise ship, even though it's always been my dream to do this!"

I shrug. "My mom likes having a second opinion, that's all. She used to run everything by my dad, but after they split up, I guess that kind of became my job."

When the elevator doors open, the hallway is in total chaos, with people running around as if the ship is sinking. Katy and I hurry toward the laundry room (it's so big they should call it the laundry *cavern*) to find my mom standing in the middle of a mound of wet pool towels. Every single one of them is pink—not cute, baby pink, but gross, dirty laundry pink. It's the same color that I managed to dye my mom's favorite white blouse after I accidentally washed it with one of my red sweaters a few months ago.

"Ainsley, there you are!" Mom cries. "Look at all this!"

"What happened?" I ask.

Mom glances at one of the laundry ladies, who shakes her head miserably. "I honestly do not know," the woman says in a thick accent that instantly makes me think of castles and vampires. Her name tag informs me that her name is Adelina. "Everything was okay, and then the water turned this color and all the white towels came out like this." She gives my mom a pleading look. "Please do not fire me."

Mom's face softens. "At least it's only the pool towels," she tells Adelina. "Maybe—"

Before she can go on, a voice booms from out in the hallway. "What in the world is going on here?"

Mom's eyes widen, and both her nostrils start to twitch. There's only one person on the ship who could make her this nervous. And sure enough, a second later, Captain Hook sweeps into the room.

Even though he's short and thin, he seems to fill the entire space.

"Captain Thomas," Mom says.

Okay, his name isn't actually Captain Hook, but I swear he wants us to think he's a pirate. If he just had a pointy beard and a hook hand, no one would think twice about it. But his custom-made hook has a compass built into the wrist—a compass!—and he always has one of those old-timey spyglass things tucked under his arm. I bet he'd carry around a sword too, if it wouldn't totally freak out the passengers. Of course, no one would ever call him Captain Hook to his face.

"I've been hearing nothing but panicked messages coming from down here. What is all this?" he demands.

"A bit of a mishap, sir, but we're taking care of it,"
Mom says.

He turns to glare at Adelina. "Can you explain
how this happened?"

She looks down at her hands and shakes her head.
"I cannot, Captain."

"Lydia?" he says, turning back to my mom. "How
are you going to fix this?"

Everyone in the room seems to be holding their
breath.

"We have people checking the pipes," Mom says
weakly. "And after that, I suppose . . ." I can see her
wracking her brain, trying to come up with an answer.
When she doesn't say anything else, the captain lets
out an annoyed sigh.

"Lydia, you were hired to make everything on this
ship run smoothly," he says. "We've only been at sea a
few hours, and already I'm getting complaints about
the staff. And now this?"

Mom's mouth opens, but no sound comes out. I

can see the defeat creeping into her shoulders, all the doubt she's been hiding from everyone but me. I can't stand to see her like that. It reminds me too much of how she was right after Dad moved out.

I keep waiting for someone else to say something, but they're all silent. "Um, excuse me, sir," I finally say, taking a tiny step forward.

The captain turns to size me up. "Yes?"

"Hi, sir. Um, I think only the pool towels are pink, and only the ones that were used today." I turn to Adelina. "That can't be that many, can it?"

"About one fourth of them," she answers.

"Can we get by with the ones we have until we get back to Florida next week?"

Adelina hesitates. "After we fix the machines, it will be hard to manage with only the regular towels . . . but not impossible."

I turn back to the captain. "And if we do have to use the pink ones," I say slowly, my brain churning, "maybe we could make it part of a theme. You know, um, like Pink Fairy Day at the kids' pool or something! I met a couple little girls this morning who would love that."

The captain seems to consider this for a moment. Then he waves his hand—his regular one—as if brushing it all aside. "Whatever the solution is, just make it happen. I don't have time to deal with this nonsense when I have a ship to run." Then he looks back at me and says, "Is that seaweed in your hair? Remember, we have standards on this vessel."

"Aye, aye, Captain Hook!" I say, trying to claw the hairnet out of my ponytail.

There's a collective gasp as I realize what I've said. Did I really just call him Captain Hook *out loud*?

I wait for him to erupt, to order me to walk the plank or something. Instead, the captain's eyes narrow, and he looks at my name tag.

"Ainsley," he reads. "That makes you Lydia's daughter, right?"

I gulp and manage a tiny nod.

He looks back at my mom. "Well," he says. "Well." Then he turns on his heel and strides out the door.

The minute he's gone, everyone sighs in relief. Everyone except for me. I can't believe it. What did I do?

"Good thinking, Ainsley," Katy says. "I would love to dress up as a pink fairy!" She's the only one who seems totally oblivious to what a huge mistake I just made.

I glance over at Mom who's still standing in the middle of the room looking a little shaken. When our eyes meet, she gives me a tight smile.

"Mom, I'm sorry. I was trying to help!"

"I know you were, and I appreciate it. He'll . . . he'll get over it. And we'll be fine, okay?"

I nod, but I can't help thinking that she's trying to convince herself more than she's trying to convince me. We've only been at sea for less than a day, and already I might have ruined my mom's chances for a fresh start. Not to mention our whole summer.

Chapter 5

I'm usually a morning person—that's the best time to photograph animals in the wild, after all—but I am definitely not ready to handle half a dozen rabid little kids at eight a.m. Their parents dumped them here right after breakfast and ran off to grab spots by the pool, so I don't even have any adults around to back mc up. On other cruise ships, there would probably be a few people manning the kids' activities, but we're pretty understaffed here. That's why all the crew members have to juggle multiple jobs all week.

The kids range in age from three to six, but they all have one thing in common. They clearly don't want to be here.

"Where's Elsa?" a little girl keeps asking me as she tugs on the hem of my shorts. "Why isn't Elsa here?" I wonder if her parents got her here by promising a visit with her favorite Disney character and then left me to break the bad news. Cowards.

"She might come later," I tell her. Yup, I'm a coward too.

I ask all the kids to gather in a circle. Five minutes later, we're in something that resembles a triangle. Good enough.

"When do we get to make a dragon?" asks a boy in an enormous blue sun hat and a long-sleeve shirt and pants that look way too hot for this humidity. He's probably the oldest kid in the bunch, and I can already tell he's going to be a handful. The minute he came into the room, he informed me that his name was Nathan and that he was from Washington, *not* the state but the nation's capital. "I had a dragon on my bed this morning, and I want to learn how to make one."

"We'll get to that," I tell him, slapping on my patented fake smile. "But today, we're going to be making . . . magical serpents!" I pull out my pathetic excuse for a snake and wave it around, as if pretending that it can fly will somehow make it look more impressive.

Nathan glares at me. "I made one of those when I was still in diapers," he informs me. "I told my parents this class would be below my ability level. Do you have any paper? I'm going to do origami."

I checked the kids' activity room—aka the Fairy Fun Zone!—when I first got here, but the drawers and cabinets were mostly empty except for some random knitting posters and brochures. The stack of towels was already waiting for me when I arrived. I couldn't help smiling when I saw all of the towels were the pink-tinged ones. I guess Adelina liked my idea of finding non-swimming uses for them.

"Sorry, kiddo," I tell him. "No origami. Just towels today."

He scowls again and grabs his towel as I turn toward the only other boy in the class, who's demanding to know why we're making "pink girl serpents."

When I glance back at Nathan, he's already made a perfect towel snake, just like the one I saw in the book.

"Okay, take your towel and smooth it out on the floor like this!" I say, trying to sound enthusiastic while ignoring the little girl who's pulling at my shorts again and chanting Elsa's name. "Then roll up one end like this!"

The kids follow my lead, and a couple of them do it right. Even Extreme Elsa Fan gives her towel a little bit of a roll. But Jorman, the other boy in the class (whose name sounds totally made-up), just sits in the corner and shakes his head. "I'm not making a pink snake," he says. "Snakes can't be girls."

"There are plenty of girl snakes!" I tell him. "And just because it's pink doesn't mean it's a girl."

"Yes, it is!" he cries. "I want to make a truck!" Then he opens his mouth and lets out a scream as if he's being murdered. All I can do is stare. I've never heard anything—not even a teakettle—make that sound before.

Instantly, the other kids start screaming too. The room fills up with so much sound, it's a miracle the window doesn't explode.

For a second, I consider sitting on the floor and screaming too. Why did I ever agree to this? What do I know about making towel sculptures or taking care of little kids?

Suddenly, the door to the activity room swings open. I whirl around, terrified that it's one of the kids' parents rushing in to save their distressed angel. Instead, it's even worse. Ian the Pig is standing in the doorway, arms crossed in front of his chest.

"Need some help?" he says. Even though he's not wearing his costume, his smirk makes him just as piggish as he was yesterday.

"Nope! I'm fine!" I cry as Jorman kicks his towel clear across the room.

Ian raises an eyebrow. "Are you sure?"

Before I can say anything back, something catches my eye.

I suck in a breath as I stare out the window. It's Cute Dwarf! He's walking by with another guy I recognize from the show. They're in waiter uniforms that are probably way too hot for this weather, but Cute Dwarf actually makes his look good.

"Pretty obsessed, aren't you?" Ian says. "You've had drool coming out of your mouth since you saw Neil yesterday."

Neil! His name is Neil! That fits him a million times better than Smith. I wish I could pump Ian for more info, but that will only prove his point.

Instead, I do my best to shrug and say, "You don't know what you're talking about." Ian doesn't look convinced.

"You sure you don't want some help?" he asks as the wailing gets even louder. "I'm pretty good with kids."

"I'm good with kids too," I insist, even though it's obviously not true. Just because I'm working on a fairy tale cruise, though, doesn't mean I need to act like a helpless maiden in need of rescuing. "I can handle it. I don't need your help."

"Geez," Ian says. "Whatever happened to 'thanks for the offer'?" He frowns, then turns and leaves the room. And I'm alone with a bunch of screaming kids again.

Okay, I can do this.

"Listen up, everyone!" I call.

No response. But the crying has to die down soon, right? Once the kids wear themselves out?

After another minute, I'm pretty sure the answer to that question is no. I have to do something fast or risk the parents coming back to find their precious snowflakes covered in tears and snot.

"If you don't want to fold towels, we don't have to fold towels!" I call. "We can do anything you want! Just name it!"

Elsa Fan stops crying and looks up at me. "Anything?"

"Um, well, within reason," I say.

"Can I watch TV?" she asks. "Mommy says I can't watch TV for the whole cruise!"

"Sure!" I point her to one of the TVs in the corner.

"Go ahead and turn it on. Just shut it off before your mom gets here, okay?"

That sure gets the other kids' attention. Another girl goes to watch TV too, while the others start bombarding me with requests.

"Can I spin around in circles on the floor?" Jorman asks.

"Um, okay," I say. "Knock yourself out. Just, you know, don't *actually* knock yourself out." All right, I'm not being the model of responsibility right now, but at least no one's crying anymore. That's something, isn't it?

Soon the kids are occupied all over the room doing stuff their parents don't want them doing, like saying bad words and picking their noses. Maybe spending every waking second with your family in the middle of the ocean makes you a little nuts.

The only person who hasn't asked me for anything is Nathan. "What do you want to do?" I ask.

He pushes his blue glasses up his nose. "I'm here to fold towels, so I want to fold towels."

"Isn't there anything your parents don't let you do?"

"Tons of stuff," he says. "But my sister always tells on me."

I glance around the room. "Is your sister here?"

"No, but she'll find out." He shrugs. "Besides, I like folding towels." He focuses on re-rolling his towel snake so that it's even more perfect than before.

"Well, if you want to make a few more of those," I say, "then the other kids will have something to take with them when we're done." And then I won't get in trouble, I silently add.

"Yeah, okay." Nathan grabs some more towels and gets to work.

And that's how we spend the next twenty minutes until the end of the class. The kids manage not to hurt themselves—although Jorman comes pretty close to spinning into the wall a few times—and I'm pretty sure one of the girls knows a lot more bad words than I do. But they all seem happy when I have them gather together again.

"So you're not going to tell your parents that I let

you do all this stuff, okay?" I say, handing out the towel snakes that Nathan made. "It'll be our secret."

They all nod and give me wide smiles.

"Will you let us punch the wall if we come tomorrow?" Jorman asks.

I swallow. For a second, I'd forgotten all about having to do this class again.

Before I can answer, the door bursts open and a couple of parents who've clearly had one too many mimosas with breakfast waltz in to pick up their kids.

"How's my little Sophia doing?" Elsa Fan's mom says.

The little girl runs over and hugs her. "Good! Look, Mommy. Elsa's sister is here!" For some reason, she points at me.

Her mom gives me a puzzled look, and I just shrug. I'm not sure how letting Sophia watch TV turned me into Disney royalty, but I'll take it.

"Oh . . . that's great, honey," the woman says. Then she starts cooing over the snake Sophia is holding.

"We'll definitely have to come back tomorrow!" she tells me.

After that, the other parents bustle in to collect their kids, and before I know it, the room is empty and quiet. Okay, so no one actually learned anything about towel folding, but at least I survived the first class in one piece. Take that, Piggy Ian. I didn't need your help after all.

Chapter 6

That afternoon before the final run-through for tonight's show, everyone's buzzing about some guy in the kitchen named Douglas getting fired.

"Once we get to Grand Turk Island tomorrow, he's supposed to get off the ship and fly back home on his own dime," one of the dwarves says.

"What did he do wrong?" I ask.

"I heard he undercooked Captain Thomas's steak," Smith says.

"No, I heard he added too much salt to the captain's stew," Gemma whispers.

"No way," Neil chimes in, and I can't help the tingle that runs through me at finally getting to hear the sound of his voice. "I heard he put poison in the captain's oatmeal."

"He'd go to jail for that," Ian jumps in, his voice flat. "The guy stole from some of the passengers. He gave the stuff back, so no one's pressing charges, but they still don't want someone like him on the ship."

"How do you know?" I ask.

Ian only shrugs and says, "It doesn't matter."

But it does matter to me. I'm already on Captain Thomas's bad side. I don't want to do something else wrong and get myself—and Mom—sent home.

When rehearsal starts, I lie on the mattress in the corner of the stage trying to look asleep while simultaneously spying on Neil from the corner of my eye. It's tricky to see him when he's offstage, but if I position my head just so, I can barely make out his—

"Briar Rose!" Stefan calls from the front row. He doesn't seem to care about learning anyone's name, so he simply refers to us by our character names. "You should be in a dead sleep! Not thrashing around like a dreaming puppy!"

"Sorry," I call back while everyone stares at me. After only a day, I'm already starting to build up quite a reputation for myself with the cast. I don't want them to think I'm only here because I'm the cruise director's daughter. After all, they had to go through actual auditions to get here. But let's face it: I *am* only here because I'm the cruise director's daughter.

The scene continues, and Gemma and Smith come onstage, acting as if they're totally in love with each other. Well, at least Gemma is acting. Smith is just standing there. Maybe Piggy Ian had a point about Smith only getting cast because of his fancy relations, but he really does look the part. Maybe no one in the audience will care that he has the charisma of a piece of dry toast.

Finally, it's time for the dwarves' finale. I keep my eyes open a slit, watching Neil prancing around at the back of the line. His knees look so *good* in tights. I didn't even know that was possible!

Then the dwarves prance offstage, and Stefan tells everyone else to clear off. "Let's run the very last scene of the final show since we've never done it before. Briar Rose! Prince Handsome! Pucker up!"

Wait. What? I sit up, suddenly feeling dazed as if I really am coming out of a deep sleep.

"I bet you've been practicing in the mirror," Smith says, making little kissy faces at me.

"We have to kiss onstage?" I whisper, horrified.

"Haven't you read the script?" Smith asks.

"Um, I haven't gotten to the end yet." The truth is, I've barely looked at it. With the rush of getting settled here and learning about my new jobs—not to mention double-checking every single thing Mom does—I really haven't had time.

"On the last night, I kiss Briar Rose, and she awakens from her deep sleep," Smith explains. Then he gives me a big wink. "Never underestimate the power of a good smooch, am I right?"

I can't believe this. My first kiss is supposed to happen onstage with the most stuck-up person I've ever met? One who thinks of me as a little kid? With Neil (and everyone else) watching?

Stefan marches over, giving us instructions that don't really make sense. "Be romantic but subdued. This is your big moment so make sure to make it shine, but don't overact. Let the moment take over, but keep track of your blocking."

"I don't have any lines, right?" I ask.

Stefan gives me a withering look. "No, you merely wake up when he kisses you, sit up, and wave to the audience. Do you think you can handle that?"

"Yes." At least, I hope I can. My palms suddenly start sweating as I have traumatizing flashbacks to my total meltdown in the second grade play. But I refuse to let that happen again, not when so much is riding on things going perfectly for Mom and me. Even if it means letting Smith kiss me. I mean, how bad can it be?

"Good. Let's run it." Stefan claps his hands for some reason and marches off.

"Don't worry," Smith tells me with a wink. "I made sure to eat an extra mint for you."

Gross. I flop back on the bed, tempted to cover myself with the blanket and pretend to be dead like

Schneewittchen. But then Stefan claps his hands again, and the scene starts.

"Who is this fair maiden?" Smith says in his lulling monotone. "She is the most beautiful creature I have ever seen. I must have one kiss."

I hold perfectly still with my eyes closed, dreading what's coming. I can smell him approaching, like a peppermint cloud. Should I pucker up? Do girls in deep, spell-induced sleeps pucker? I decide to stay frozen.

Smith's breath hits my face, and then what feels like two slugs mash down on my lips. I almost scream as Smith pulls away.

My eyes fly open, and I scramble to sit up. Is that what kissing is like? *Blargh!*

"The maiden lives!" Smith says, his monotone suddenly at full volume. "It is truly a happy ending!"

Then he turns to me, and I realize he's expecting me to do something. Is he gearing up for another kiss? No way! I don't care if Stefan threatens to throw me overboard. I am never letting those slug lips near me again!

"Wave!" Stefan yells. "Why aren't you waving?"

Right. My one part in the play.

I look out at the audience and give a limp wave while Smith puts a too-tight arm around my waist. When I try to smile at the audience, I spot a frowning face near the side door. Captain Thomas. He's holding his spyglass up to his eye, as if he's trying to spot land on the horizon. Except his pirate contraption isn't fixed on some distant island. It's aimed right at me.

Oh no. Did he just see my miserable performance? He already hates me, and now he's watching me ruin the finale of what's supposed to be the biggest show of the entire cruise?

"Sorry!" I tell Stefan. "I'll do better this time!" I cringe at the thought of kissing Smith again, but I have to save face in front of Captain Thomas. He can't see Lydia's daughter messing up again.

"Forget it," Stefan says. "We have more important scenes to run. We'll just do it during the last show. Think you can handle that?" He's looking at me as if

I'm a total imbecile. Honestly, I'm starting to feel like one.

"I can. I promise."

As I scurry off the stage, I realize Captain Thomas isn't pointing his spyglass at me anymore. Instead, he and Piggy Ian seem to be having some sort of debate in the back of the theater. For a second, hope flashes through my chest. Maybe the captain is firing him too! But then I feel awful for thinking it. As annoying as he is, Ian hasn't done anything that would make me wish he'd lose his job. Still, there's something about him that rubs me the wrong way.

Smith waltzes up to me in the wings. "I'm happy to help you with your acting skills anytime," he says before sauntering off. The idea is so ridiculous that I actually stick my tongue out.

As I pull off my wig and drop it on the costume table, I hear a guy clear his throat behind me. I turn to find Neil dawdling in the wings, almost as if he's waiting to talk to me.

"Hey!" he says. Oh my gosh. He really is here to talk to me!

"Um, hi," I say, barely above a whisper.

He opens his mouth to reply, but then—

"Ainsley!" someone calls out from the edge of the stage. It's Katy, dressed in her mermaid costume, as usual, and furiously waving to me. "Quick, follow me."

I glance at Neil, but he's already walking away. Ugh.

"Let me guess," I say as I follow Katy off the stage. "My mom needs my help with something again."

"Not exactly," Katy says. "But she's locked herself in the meat room and won't come out. Adelina asked me to get you before Captain Thomas finds out and . . ."

Katy doesn't need to finish the sentence. We both know what would happen. I don't wait for her to waddle along beside me. There's no time for that. Instead, I take off at a run.

Chapter 7

Mom, what is it? What happened?"

It took me about five minutes to convince her to even open the door to the cold storage room. Now that I'm in it, I'm really wishing I brought a jacket.

Mom is sitting on an enormous bucket of salad dressing with her head in her hands, hair sticking out through her fingers in wavy spikes. I guess she didn't take the time to blow-dry it this morning. That's not a good sign.

After Dad moved out, Mom stopped drying her hair in the mornings, which I noticed right away because she's been styling it religiously every day since I can remember. Then she stopped ironing her clothes, so she'd go to work looking as if she'd just rolled out of bed. Then she stopped answering the phone, so I'd have to take down messages and pester her to call people back unless it was easier to do it myself.

After a few months of that, Mom lost her job at the real estate office where she worked. She kept saying she was looking for a new job, but I was the one really looking—and paying bills and cooking meals and doing whatever else she needed me to. If her friend hadn't called about the cruise ship opening, I don't know what would have happened. But the minute we got on the ship, Mom's hair was sleek and straight again, and her clothes were perfectly pressed. Even her shoes were shined. I'd let myself hope that she was back to her old self and that I could be an average kid again.

But maybe it was too good to be true.

"What was I thinking, Ains? I can't do this job. I'm too out of practice."

"But we only just started!" I say. "Of course things are going to be a little rough at first. It'll get better once we get the hang of everything." I realize that I sound just like my dad used to whenever Mom would start doubting herself. "Did something happen?"

Mom lets out a long sigh and hands me a piece of paper covered in crowded handwriting.

"*People aren't purchasing the photos at Enchanted Reflections*," I read. "*No one's set foot in the Oven Lounge and Nightclub. No vegan entrees at the Lost Children Dining Room.*" I flip the paper over and see the writing goes on for another page. "Mom, what is this?"

"The captain wanted to see me this morning," she says. "He gave me a list of all the things that are already going wrong. And he wants them all resolved by the time we get back to Fort Lauderdale."

The list suddenly seems to double in weight in my hand. "How are we supposed to do all of this in only five days?"

"Some of them are small fixes, but the big ones he listed can't be taken care of in so little time!" Mom says. And that's when I see it, that look of defeat that I saw after Dad moved out, and again after Mom lost her real estate job. Before she started to fall apart.

"Don't worry," I say. "I'll figure it out."

"No, Ains," she says quietly, taking the list from me and slipping it in her pocket. "It's not your job. It's mine. I'll make it work. Okay?"

She thinks she means it. And honestly, I wish I could believe her. I'd much rather hang out with Katy and the other mermaids and try talking to Neil than help my mom save this sinking ship. But I'm afraid if I don't help, our fresh start at sea will be over by the end of our first week. Now that I finally have my old mom back, I can't let her turn into a pajama shut-in again.

"Okay, Mom," I say. "Things will get better. I promise."

She gets to her feet and pulls open the door. Just in time too, since my toes are starting to go numb.

"You know what I wish we could do more than anything right now?" she says. "Watch a terrible movie." She sighs. "I can't believe we're missing a whole summer of blockbusters. We'll have a lot of catching up to do when we get home."

It might sound weird, but Mom and I love watching disaster movies together. It's been our thing since I was really little. The movies are always so ridiculous and over-the-top that we laugh through them. Dad would always lock himself in his study during movie nights so he wouldn't have to listen to us acting out the cheesy dialogue.

"I know! I can't wait to see the sequel to that one about all the bridges in the world collapsing. What's it called?" I ask as we head down the corridor.

"*A Bridge Two Far*," Mom says in a melodramatic voice. Then she pulls her wild hair into a ponytail. "Do I look okay? I should have blow-dried my hair today. I swear my curls get bigger every time I look at them."

"You look fine. At least you don't look like a drowned rat. The humidity is making my hair stringier than ever."

"At least you can brush through yours," she says.

"At least yours is an actual color instead of—"

"*Blah-brown*," she finishes for me, rolling her eyes like she always does when we have this conversation.

Then she gives me a hug. "Thanks, Ains. I'm so glad you're here with me. You are my rock."

I pull away. *My rock*. That's what she used to call Dad. Mom always said that he was the one who kept her grounded, and I guess now that's my job. But I don't feel like anyone's rock. I barely even feel like a pebble.

After dropping Mom off at her office so she can pull herself together before her next meeting, I pass Enchanted Reflections, the photo kiosk that was on the captain's list. It's where people have their pictures taken in front of silly fairy tale backdrops.

I hover behind a column, watching the guy behind the camera as he tries to get a set of toddler triplets to sit long enough to have their picture taken in front of a cartoony castle. The photographer, whose name is "Mitch!" according to his name tag, is barely holding the camera the right way, and he's totally at the wrong angle. He'll probably wind up getting shots of only the kids' foreheads instead of their faces, and I seriously doubt the parents will want to buy prints of those. No wonder the kiosk is in so much trouble.

Mitch! accidentally drops a lens cap, and it rolls toward my feet. He mutters something under his breath before going to retrieve it. I grab it and hold it out to him.

"Thanks," he says, giving me a tired smile. One of the triplets lets out an angry scream behind him, and Mitch! sets his jaw and straightens his shoulders as if he's about to go into battle. I wonder if the exclamation point after his name is a way to remind himself to be excited about his job.

As he turns back to them, I catch his elbow. "Wait," I say, before I can stop myself. "Um, you might want to angle the camera down. Also, sometimes it helps to lie on your belly with really little kids." I haven't done pictures of a lot of children, but I use that technique with small animals and it works really well.

For a second, I'm afraid he'll be offended that a complete stranger is giving him advice, but he smiles and says, "Thanks. I'll try that." Then he goes back and immediately spreads out on his stomach.

I head out to the walking track, hoping it's still quiet because of the paint smell. Sadly, it's as crowded here as on the rest of the ship. I never realized before how much I like being alone, but having people around me all the time is bringing out my inner loner. No wonder Mom locked herself in the cold storage room.

As I lean against the railing, some movement in the water catches my eye. I scramble to get my camera out of my pocket. Maybe I'll get to photograph a dolphin, or even a whale! But when I zoom in with my lens, I realize it's only a clump of trash floating around in the ocean. Gross.

I sigh and head to the top deck, where people are milling around the pool and bopping to the live music (played by a mariachi band in gnome costumes, for some reason). I'm about to duck inside and go get ready for dinner duty again, before my—gulp—big stage debut tonight, when I notice a supersized mole on an old man's hairy back.

I cringe at the sight, but I know Alyssa will murder me if I don't get a shot. I take out my camera, make sure no one is watching, and then quickly snap a couple of pictures.

As I'm shoving the camera back into my pocket, I spot Neil near the pool. My whole body freezes. I stand there staring at him as if moving might scare him away.

He and one of the other dwarves from the show are cleaning up empty cups and used napkins left behind by the people hanging out by the pool. I can't help noticing how bored he looks, not that I can blame him. I only hope one of the Spies doesn't catch him looking anything less than thrilled, or he might get into trouble.

As I—let's face it—spy on him, I can't help marveling at how cute Neil is. There's something so confident about the way he moves, as if he's not afraid of making a total fool out of himself. I bet he'd never accidentally call Captain Thomas the wrong name to his face.

Neil doesn't even glance in my direction. You'd think being in the middle of the ocean with a guy would make it easy to get him to notice you, but the ship is so jam-packed with people that I'm probably just another face in the crowd.

If Mom and I don't figure out a way to make things work here, I might never get a chance to actually talk to him.

Chapter 8

The show starts in five minutes, and I'm freaking out. I don't have any lines—don't even have to *do* anything besides pretend to be asleep—but all I can think about is that stupid play in second grade. My parents assured me that I'd never have to set foot onstage again if I didn't want to, and I'd managed to avoid it ever since. Until now.

How did I let my mom talk me into this?

"Hey, are you okay?" Smith asks, coming up to me.

"I don't know," I admit, surprised he actually cares.

"You're not going to throw up or something, are you?" He takes a step back.

I shake my head, hoping it's true.

"Okay, in that case, can you move over? You're kind of blocking my view."

I blink and realize that I'm standing in front of a full-length mirror. "Oh, sorry." I shuffle even farther into the corner while Smith plants himself in front of the mirror and starts making kissy faces at his reflection.

"Three minutes!" the stage manager calls, and my breath catches in my chest. I can't do this. I should make a run for it now and save everyone a lot of embarrassment.

I turn to flee and—*thunk!*—smack into none other than Piggy Ian again.

"Don't you ever watch where you're going?" he cries, tearing off his pig head.

"Me?" I say, rubbing my forehead. "You're the one who keeps slamming that enormous skull of yours into me. I probably have a concussion thanks to you."

"Two minutes!" the stage manager calls.

I must look panicked because Ian's expression suddenly changes. "Hey, are you okay?"

"Don't worry. I won't throw up on you," I mutter, but I'm really not so sure this time.

"All right. Let's get you onstage." He sticks his pig head back on and holds his elbow out as if he's going to escort me.

"Um . . ." My feet are still screaming at me to run, but Piggy Ian is blocking my way.

"Places!" the stage manager is calling. "Places, everyone!"

"Come on," Ian says. "We have to go." Then he clamps my wrist with his furry paw and practically deposits me onto the mattress in the corner of the stage. "Break a leg," I think I hear him whisper before he disappears behind the bushes on the other side of the stage, but I'm too petrified to say anything back.

Instead, I lie sprawled on the mattress, paralyzed as I hear the murmur of the crowd on the other side of the curtain. All of a sudden, I'm back in elementary school, when I stepped forward to say my one line and blanked. I stood there, totally frozen, thinking about how much I was disappointing the teacher and the other kids and, most importantly, my parents, who were both sitting in the front row. And finally, when I opened my mouth to say something, I burst into tears instead. Then I ran off the stage and refused to go back on.

That disaster was in front of an audience of only about fifty people. There are *way* more than that here tonight. Dozens. Hundreds. *Thousands.*

The thought is too much, and I start to feel so woozy that all I can do is close my eyes. As I hear the faint sound of the curtain opening for Act I and feel the heat of the stage lights as they come on, everything around me goes black.

"I can't believe you fainted!" Katy says, laughing as I tell her about my big stage debut. We're squished on her bed in our pajamas, having the cruise equivalent of a slumber party. One perk of having a roommate is getting to dish with someone at the end of a crazy day.

"Luckily no one noticed," I say.

Katy giggles. "Everyone probably thought you were really committing to your character."

I hide my face in a pillow, my cheeks hot from embarrassment. I didn't wake up until about halfway through the play. Thankfully, I didn't startle awake and bolt up in bed. Instead, reality slowly seeped back in, and I somehow managed to keep it together for the rest of the show. I guess I sort of have Piggy Ian to thank for that. If he hadn't dragged me onstage, I don't think I would have made it there at all.

"At least the audience seemed to like the show, from what I could see." Even when I wasn't passed out from fright, it was still hard to watch the performance when my eyes were supposed to be closed.

"I heard people raving about the Pig King and Lady Lovely dance," Katy says.

"They got a standing ovation!" That was the big shocker of the night. From the snippets I saw of Piggy Ian and his partner, a quiet girl named Faria, prancing across the stage, I had to admit they were really good. I actually believed the two of them were their characters, unlike Smith, who was just Smith dressed up to look like a prince. "Too bad Smith is more Pinocchio than prince."

"He's not so bad," Katy says softly.

I laugh. "If this cruise ship thing doesn't work out, he might have a career in Hollywood ahead of him. Maybe they'll cast him in some cruise ship disaster movie!"

I expect Katy to giggle at the idea, but she's suddenly gone oddly quiet as she fusses with the hem of her pajama pants.

"What's wrong?" I ask.

"Um, so . . . you and Smith are pretty close, right?" she says, still not looking at me.

"Not by choice," I say, shuddering at the memory of his slug lips on mine. "Why?"

"I was wondering if you thought he might like someone like me."

I stare at her blankly for a second before what she's saying sinks in. Then I almost fall off the bed. "Wait, you like Smith?" What is it about being stuck in the middle of the ocean that makes everyone start going gaga over one another? Myself included, I guess.

"Shh!" Katy looks around as if paparazzi might jump out of the walls. "Don't tell anyone. I don't know if I really like him yet, but he's been smiling at me a lot since we got on board. I've only talked to him about my dog, though. I was too nervous to say anything else!"

"You really like him?" I can't help asking. "He's so—"

"Cute?" Katy chirps. "And talented. And heavenly! Even his hair is like a halo around his head."

I choke back a laugh. Katy is really serious. "He'd be a fool not to like you," I tell her, and I mean it.

She gives me a bright smile and flops back on her bed. "You should have come out with the mermaids tonight. We'd find you your very own hottie in no time!"

"I was too tired after the show," I say. So far, every day of the cruise has felt about a month long. "And anyway, there's already someone I kind of like." It's weird to confide in someone other than Alyssa and Brooke, but I find myself spilling everything about Neil—the soulful stare we exchanged and the notebook and how cute his knees look in tights . . .

Katy's eyes get bigger and bigger as I tell her about him. "It's like destiny, the two of you winding up on this ship together. So romantic! You have to talk to him!"

"Trust me. I'm working on it."

Chapter 9

Not long after the sun comes up, I hear a soft knock at the door. Resting against the doorframe is a package from Mom, along with a note.

I had a great idea for a new name for the Oven Nightclub! If we want it to be a teen hot spot, let's call it the Hot Spot! Can you do me a favor and put this temporary sign above the door before your class this morning? Thanks, Ains! You're the best!

She's included a taped-together paper sign that she clearly made on her computer and printed out. I guess when she says "temporary," she means it. I'm not sure the sign or the new name will help get people my age to check out the club, but if Mom is excited about it then I'll give it a try. That's what you do when you're someone's rock, right?

I get dressed, grab the towel-folding book, and sneak out of the room without waking Katy up. Then I walk through the ship, enjoying the rare quiet and snapping pictures of the water, the clouds, and even some of the ship. Now that everything's freshly painted, it actually looks pretty good.

When I get to the Oven, I decide to go inside and grab a smoothie before I get to work. The place is completely empty, but it still takes the guy behind the counter, whose name tag says "Matthieu," forever to make my drink. When I take a sip, though, I actually gasp.

"This is amazing!"

"Merci!" Matthieu says in a thick French accent as he tucks one of his dreadlocks back into his ponytail. "Blueberry, mango, and peanut butter swirl. I made it special for you."

I laugh. "If the smoothies are so good, why doesn't

anyone come here?" I look around at the cozy couches. This looks like the perfect place to hang out.

Matthieu subtly nods toward one of the Spies in the corner who's scanning the room like she's looking for troublemakers.

"Yeah, I guess having people like that around isn't the best way to get kids my age to hang out somewhere," I whisper. "Maybe we could put up some more decorations, liven things up a little." The place is pretty bare, and even though the couches are nice, there's not much to do besides hang out and wait for your smoothie. No video games or TVs or anything. And the horrible show tunes playing over the speakers aren't helping.

"We do what they tell us," he says. "And they say keep it as is."

"Well, you'll be getting a new name today," I tell him, and then explain about my mom's plan. He looks as skeptical about the idea as I feel. "Maybe I could put up some more decorations to go with the theme."

Technically, Mom only told me to put up a sign, but she didn't say anything about *not* putting up other things, right?

Matthieu shrugs. "There's colored paper under the counter, if you want to use it."

A couple crew members come in, and Matthieu starts making more smoothies while I quickly cut out some paper palm trees and other tropical shapes. When I put them up on the walls, they definitely look cheesy, but at least they help add a little color to the place.

"Ready to hang up a sign?" someone says in my ear.

I spin around to find Piggy Ian standing behind me, grinning that obnoxious grin of his.

"Excuse me?"

"Your mom asked me to come help you." He holds up a stepladder, and I realize that as much as I want to tell him I don't need his help (again), I actually can't put up the Hot Spot sign without it.

"Fine. Let's go," I say.

When we're outside, I grab the ladder from Ian and climb up to slap the sign over the club's entrance. Too late, I realize that I forgot to put tape on the back of the paper first. He seems to be able to read my mind, though, because he hands up some pre-rolled pieces. Ugh.

"Thanks," I mutter.

"You really don't like people helping you, do you?" Ian asks, holding the ladder steady.

"That's not true. I let you practically push me out onstage last night, didn't I?" I clear my throat. "Which . . . by the way . . . thanks. I . . . I owe you." I hate to admit it, but if Ian hadn't been there, I'd probably still be hyperventilating in the wings.

"Will you be okay for the show tonight?" he asks.

"I'll be fine," I insist, but the truth is, I have no idea. And judging by his raised eyebrows, he can tell that I'm lying. I finish hanging up the sign and climb back down. "Well, see ya," I say.

"Wait!" Ian calls after me. "How about a trade? I

make sure you're onstage when you're supposed to be, and you help me run lines."

"Isn't that what Faria is for?" From what I've seen, the girl playing Lady Lovely opposite his Pig King is a great actress and dancer.

"Have you ever heard her talk outside of the play?" he asks. When I shake my head, he says, "Exactly. She refuses to speak except when she's onstage. So unless we're at rehearsal or in the show, she won't open her mouth."

"I don't really have time," I say, which is true. It's also true that I'd really rather not spend any more time with Piggy Ian than necessary.

"Come on, please?" he says, and I'm surprised at how desperate he sounds. "I can't mess this up. The more I practice, the better."

Wow, he sounds like he means it. "Fine," I say. "You help me and I help you."

"Awesome!" he says. "See you back here after your class?"

"Wait, we're starting right away?"

"If you haven't noticed, stuff happens really fast on this ship," he says. "You've gotta keep up." Then he does a dorky finger-gun thing at me, complete with *pew pew pew* sounds as if he's a cowboy or something, before he disappears out the door. Ugh.

I duck back into the Hot Spot to grab the towel-folding book and freeze when I spot Neil settling in on one of the couches with his Moleskine notebook.

He's only a few feet away from me! I have to get a picture of him to show Alyssa and Brooke. I hold my breath and then oh-so-subtly take my camera out of my pocket and snap a picture. He leans back in his seat, and I dive behind a decorative column.

For a second, I consider going over to talk to him, but I totally chicken out. Instead, I start to sneak away. But then I see Neil waving me over, a big smile on his face. I can't believe it. He actually wants to talk to me.

With the towel-folding book hugged to my chest like armor, I bravely venture the few steps over to him and mumble, "Neil? Um, hi."

"Hey! How are things going?" he says.

"Good. How about you?"

"Good!"

"You're Lydia's daughter, right? Ashley?"

"Ainsley."

"Right. Ainsley." He gives me a sparkling smile.

There's a long pause, and I scramble to come up with something interesting to say. Finally, I point to his notebook and ask, "What are you writing in there?"

Please say song lyrics. Please say song lyrics!

"Vocabulary words," he says.

Oh. "Like for an English test?" Is he doing summer school? I didn't know you could do that in the middle of the ocean.

He laughs. "No, for the SATs. I memorize lists and then write them from memory."

"Any good words today?" I ask, desperate to keep the conversation going.

He glances at his list. "The newest ones are *tangent*, *blatant*, and *plethora*."

"Oh, those are easy. 'My roommate Katy goes on a plethora of blatant tangents about her dog, Snoopy.'"

Wait. Did I just try to wow him with my vocabulary skills?

Amazingly, he doesn't point at me and yell, "Nerd!" Instead, he says, "Maybe you could help me study sometime."

"Really?" He wants me, a junior high student, to help him with his SAT words?

"Sure," he says, smiling again. "You seem pretty smart. Besides, I've been wanting to get to know you better."

"Y-you have?"

His smile widens. "Totally. Maybe we could—"

But he doesn't have a chance to finish because at that moment the Spy who was staked out in the corner comes over and hisses, "Ainsley Parker, aren't you supposed to be teaching a class right now?"

Gah! How do they *do* that? I don't think I've ever

seen this woman before today. How does she know who I am? And why did she have to interrupt right when it sounded as if Neil might actually ask me out on a date?

"Sorry, I have to go," I tell Neil, hoping he sees how very sorry I am.

Chapter 10

As I rush toward the Fairy Fun Zone, I can't help wishing I'd never agreed to do the silly towel-folding class. Neil and I could be sitting around drinking smoothies and chatting right now.

When I get to the class, I'm expecting the turnout to be about the same as yesterday—or smaller, considering the fact that a lot of people will be heading ashore later today. Instead, the same kids have all returned, and they've brought friends. Their parents look relieved when I show up. In fact, they can't seem to get out of there fast enough. I guess spending all that time with your kids can be a little much.

"We heard we could do anything we wanted in this class!" a little boy with a mop of orange curls says. "Can we have a food fight?"

Uh-oh. "Do you have any food?" I ask him.

His face falls. "No."

"I don't either. Maybe we'll just stick with towel folding, okay?" I turn to the group and call out, "We're making magic mice today, everyone!"

Before I went to sleep last night, I practiced making a few of the easiest shapes in the towel-folding book. I finally decided on a mouse, since it only took me three tries to make it look right.

"Mice?" Nathan says, adjusting his sun hat. Once again, he's in long sleeves and pants even though I'm sweating in shorts. Maybe he's part reptile or something and can't regulate his body temperature. "What's magical about mice?"

"Didn't you ever see *Cinderella*?" I ask, biting my lip the minute the words are out of my mouth. I can't believe I just used one of the Forbidden Names! I guess I'm still a little frazzled after my conversation with Neil.

"I'm not allowed to watch anything that's not educational," Nathan says.

Meanwhile, Jorman, the one who insisted that snakes couldn't be girls, chimes in with, "That movie's for girls."

"And mice are for babies!" Nathan adds.

I sigh. "What about rats? Are rats better than mice?"

The orange-haired boy looks uncertain. "Maybe."

"Yes," Nathan chimes in. "Rats are very intelligent."

"Well, then, we're making rats," I announce.

"Are they magical rats?" Sophia asks in a quivering voice. Apparently, the idea of rats being magical terrifies her.

"Nope, not magical," I say. "They're friendly rats. Super rats! They can talk, and they know how to build things, and they help other animals because they were part of a scientific experiment that made them really smart." I realize I'm describing the plot of *Mrs. Frisby and the Rats of NIMH*, one of my favorite books when I was younger. I'd have my dad read it to me over and over.

"Rats are filthy!" another girl cries. "My grandpa says they carry diseases."

Sophia's eyes get very round. "I don't want to get sick."

"No, these are *pretend* rats," I try to explain, but no one's listening to me anymore.

"I'm allergic to animal dander," Nathan announces. "I could stop breathing if I'm around it."

"You'd *die*?" Sophia says. "My hamster died. I don't want Nathan to die!" Then she starts to scream. And the other kids start to scream. And this time, I really might scream too.

Then a miracle happens. Neil walks by and peers into the activity center window. He slows down as our eyes meet through the glass.

And then he speeds up and disappears around the corner.

Huh. Did he not see how desperate I am for some help? No, I decide. He must have not seen me. Maybe there was a glare on the window from the outside or something. Otherwise, he would have poked his head in and at least offered to help.

I guess I'm really on my own. Which is fine. I'm no damsel in distress, right? I can figure this out.

"Okay! Okay!" I say, flailing my arms and trying to calm everyone down. "No rats! We won't do rats! We'll do whatever you want! Anything!"

That, apparently, is the magic word. The kids stop freaking out, and before I know it, they've pulled all the cushions off the chairs and are having the hugest pillow fight in cruise ship history. I rush around the room, making sure no one is getting hit too hard or smothered in the chaos.

Yet again, Nathan doesn't join in. "Too many dust mites in pillows," he says. I actually feel kind of bad for the kid but also grateful that he's willing to make another batch of towel animals for everyone. Instead of rodents, he makes lobsters. They come out perfectly.

By the end of the class, the kids are exhausted. "Wow," one father says as he practically scrapes his son off the floor. "I've never seen kids so happy after a craft activity. You really know what you're doing!"

I force that smile onto my face and silently hand over the towel lobster that his son "made," trying to tell myself that I'm not a big ol' fake.

Chapter 11

You can sit right there," Ian says, pointing to an armchair in the corner of the Hot Spot. Despite this morning's name change and décor boost, it looks like the only people who hang out here are the crew members. I have yet to see a single passenger inside. At least that means it's a nice, quiet spot, and the perfect place for me to help Ian run through his scenes where no one has to see me embarrassing myself.

"So where do we start?" I ask, plopping down.

"This scene." He slides over a script that's covered in scribbles and crossed out notes. "Stefan keeps changing his mind about the lines and the blocking. That's why I want to run over the newest stuff a couple more times. Let's go from here." He points to the middle of the page and then starts doing his lines from memory.

We go back and forth like that for a few minutes, Ian acting and me reading the lines from my chair. I have to admit that Ian is really good. I actually believe that he's the Pig King. He even makes his body look kind of pig-like as he walks around.

"Okay, on your feet," he says when we're done running through the lines. "The whole scene takes place while the two characters are dancing, so we should try it that way."

"Um, what?" I sink backward into my chair. "You asked me to help you run lines. Dancing wasn't part of the deal." I glance around the lounge, mortified at the thought of anyone seeing me tripping over my own feet, but the place is as empty as ever. Not even Matthieu or any of the other employees are around. They're probably napping in the back room.

"Besides, how can I read from the script and dance at the same time?" I add.

"You only have a few lines. You'll be fine." He

grasps my hands and pulls me out of the chair. "Sorry, kid. I need a waltzing partner, and you're it."

"Don't call me 'kid.' How old are you anyway?"

"Thirteen," he says, pushing a couple end tables out of the way.

"Wait, really? You're my age?" (Almost.) "How did you get a job on board when you're not sixteen?" Most cruise lines require employees to be at least eighteen, which is why Katy and so many of the other teenagers on the ship came to work here instead.

"How did you?" He lines up my arms so that they're in waltzing position.

"I asked you first."

He ignores me and starts humming the music under his breath. Then we start waltzing, and I mean really waltzing, as if we're on one of those dancing-with-famous-people TV shows. Even though I have no idea what I'm doing and it's not easy to keep your balance when the floor is rocking under you, Ian leads so well that I barely trip over his feet or mine. As we twirl around the room, we start running lines, and I'm amazed that I'm able to remember them without the script after all.

When we're done, Ian steps back and actually applauds. "Not bad," he says. "Maybe they should have you dance in the show."

I snort. "Trust me, sleeping onstage is about all I can handle." And then for some reason, I find myself telling him about the time I burst into tears during the second grade production of *Rumpelstiltskin*.

"Shh," Ian says in a dramatic whisper. "You're not supposed to use names like that, remember?"

"Oh yeah," I whisper back with a laugh. "Sorry. I mean Whuppity Stoorie." Yup, that's the Scottish version of Rumpelstiltskin. In the Scottish tale, the character is a tricksy fairy instead of a weird little guy. The woman who plays her on the ship is barely my height and keeps her head down all the time—probably in embarrassment—so she looks even shorter.

"Anyway," Ian says. "That was years ago. Maybe you'd be better now."

I shake my head. "Trust me. I was freaking out onstage last night, and all I had to do was pretend to be asleep." I don't mention the fact that I actually passed out for part of it. Definitely too embarrassing to admit.

"You just have to practice. I used to be really shy, but I love performing, so I didn't let that stop me."

"But you make it look so easy!" I say. "You're a total natural."

He shrugs. "I want to be on Broadway and stuff when I'm older, but it takes a lot of work. You pretty much have to be perfect. That's why I hate seeing someone like Smith getting this big chance at the lead in the show when he hasn't even practiced at all."

I remember that first day when I thought Ian was such a snob for saying bad stuff about Smith, but I guess he has a point. "Is that why you're so serious about running lines?"

"Yeah, and because of my dad. He's not too happy about me wanting to go into theater, says I'll need a real career when I grow up. I'm hoping this summer will convince him."

Suddenly, a woman comes into the Hot Spot and starts looking at the smoothie menu. Not only do I notice her because she's the only non-employee here, but she also has a really interesting scar on her elbow. It looks like a smiley face.

Before I know it, my camera is in my hand, and I'm covertly snapping pictures through a nearby fern.

"What are you doing?" Ian asks, trying to look at my camera screen.

"Shh!" I wave him away. When I'm sure I've gotten a good shot, I put the camera away. "Sorry, I'm working on a project."

"On elbows?"

"No, on moles and scars. It's for my friend back home. She's had this collection going for years."

"Interesting. So you're really into photography, huh? I always see you with that camera."

"Yeah, I like taking pictures of animals—birds and

seals and stuff. Way better than photographing body parts."

"That sounds hard," he says. "Don't animals usually run or fly away before you can get a good shot?"

"Mostly, yeah, but sometimes, if you're really quiet, it's like you're not there, and they do what they would do if they were all alone. I guess those are the best pictures of people too. The ones that don't look fake."

He nods. "Yeah, I hate fake people. I can always tell when someone's putting on an act."

"Is that why you're always so blunt?" I can't help asking.

"You're one to talk!" he says, laughing. He looks at the clock, and his smile fades. "Well, thanks for your help. I should get to my real rehearsal."

"No problem."

"You should come watch. The dwarves are going to be there." He gives my side a little jab with his elbow. "One dwarf in particular."

"Shut up!" I cry, pushing him away.

"You could wow him with your dancing," Ian says in a singsong voice. "Sweep him off his pointy feet!"

"You're so immature," I say, rolling my eyes, but I can't help smiling a little.

Chapter 12

Thanks to Ian's help, I manage to get through another night of the show, and it feels like a miracle. I do spend the whole time nearly hyperventilating on the mattress, but hopefully it just looks like my sleep-breathing is very deep and steady.

Backstage after the show, Katy comes scurrying in. For once, she's not wearing her fish tail, and I'm actually kind of surprised to see that she has legs.

"Ainsley, there you are!"

"Let me guess. My mom's looking for me?" It's been over twenty-four hours since the last crisis. I figured the calm wouldn't last.

"She's waiting for you at the Oven," Katy says. "Or the Hot Spot. Whatever it's called now."

I start to rush away, but Katy grabs my elbow. "Hold on a second," she adds. "Um, can you do me a favor?"

Seriously? Do I have "ask me for a favor" written on my forehead? "What's up?" I ask.

Katy glances around and then whispers, "I'm supposed to judge a cannonball competition at the pool at noon tomorrow, but I heard Smith say he was going to be working out then. So I was thinking if I go to the gym while he's there, maybe I can get a chance to talk to him again. So . . . will you judge the competition for me?"

"Won't they notice that I'm not a mermaid?"

"You can dress up in your Briar Rose outfit. No one will care. They love princesses!"

I hesitate. The last thing I want is to get in trouble for being in the wrong place.

"Please, Ainsley?" Katy tucks her hands up like little paws and puts on her best pleading puppy face. "I'll be your best cruise friend?"

I can't help laughing. "You already are my best cruise friend." If she's really so into Smith and his slug lips, I guess I could help her out. "Okay, fine. I'll see what I can do."

"Thank you!" Katy cries with a squeal. "You're the best!"

When I get to the Hot Spot, I hope to see the place hopping. And it is . . . kind of.

But it's not full of kids. It's scattered with people of all ages wandering around with their tablets and cell phones, all looking confused.

"I thought there would be free Wi-Fi here," I hear a woman say to her friend. "It says it's a hot spot."

"Maybe it's broken. Let's ask the people at the bar." They go over to where Matthieu and a couple of other frazzled employees are trying to explain why they don't serve alcohol and why there's no free internet access.

"This place stinks," a man tells his wife. "It's like it was made for kids or something. And what's with the palm trees?" They leave, looking disgusted.

I go over to Mom who's in the corner with her face in her hands. "I don't get it," she says. "In my old cruise ship days, I had every club filled to capacity. Maybe I've lost my touch."

"No, you haven't," I assure her. "You can't get everything right on the first try, that's all."

She sighs. "I'll figure out a way to fix this . . . somehow. Maybe we can have a sock hop!"

I fight back a groan. No one my age would want to go to a sock hop. But Mom is already seriously doubting herself, so I have to be supportive. "Yeah, maybe," I say. "Is this why you had Katy find me?"

She shakes her head. "Captain Thomas asked to see us in a few minutes."

A chill goes through me. "Both of us?"

"I'm sure it's nothing to worry about," she says, almost as if she's trying to convince herself. She glances at her watch. "Come on. We don't want to be late."

When we get to Captain Thomas's office, I expect to find a dimly lit maze of telescopes and star charts . . . and I'm totally right. The only thing I wasn't imagining was a huge fish tank in the corner of the room with nothing but a small octopus inside. The creature is about the size of my head, but it's actually weirdly cute. That doesn't mean the captain hasn't trained it to be an aquatic assassin or something, so I make sure to keep my distance.

"There you are," he says. "Sit." He waves us toward a couple of chairs with his hook hand, making the compass inside it spin. I have to say that in the dim lighting, it looks pretty cool. I suddenly feel as if we're actually in a pirate movie.

"First off, I should tell you that Pink Fairy Pool Time was a big success," he says. "We've had a lot of positive reviews from passengers."

"Oh good!" Mom says. She pats my hand. "Nice thinking, Ains."

For a second, Captain Thomas gives me something that might even count as a smile, and I actually start to relax. But then his lips curl downward, and he adds, "But there are some other matters we need to discuss."

I swallow so hard, it makes my throat hurt.

"All right," Mom says softly, her nostrils twitching like crazy.

"It's come to my attention, Lydia, that your daughter has not been following the rules."

"Wh-what?" I sputter. All I've been doing since I stepped foot on this ship is following rules!

"I've been informed that you've been using your camera while you're on duty," the captain says. "There have been reports of you breaking protocol and photographing passengers."

My jaw sags open. I want to deny it, but I can't. Because it's true. All those pictures I've been taking of moles and scars for Alyssa! I thought I was being sneaky, but clearly not sneaky enough.

I'm not the only one who's broken the rules. He's singling me out because he hates me. I know it! If I hadn't called him Captain Hook to his face, he would have let this whole camera thing slide.

"Do you have any proof?" Mom asks him.

"If Ainsley would be willing to hand her camera

over for inspection, I think we'll see that the allegations are true."

"You don't have to," Mom tells me, but I sigh and pull it out of my pocket. If I refuse to show it to him, I'll look guilty. Maybe he'll appreciate that I'm being honest. Aren't pirates all about honor?

Captain Thomas takes the camera from me and flips through a few of the pictures. His lips get thinner and thinner as he goes. Finally, he stops and his eyes widen. I bet he's looking at all the pictures I've sneakily taken of moles and scars and thinking what a weirdo I am.

"I think it's best if I hang on to this for now," he says, turning my camera off and sliding it into a desk drawer.

"What?" I cry. "You can't do that! That's my property."

"We have strict codes of conduct on this ship for a reason. Any breach can be dangerous to the passengers and the crew."

"Captain, please—" Mom says, but I can hear her

voice quivering. I realize she's as scared of him as everyone else is. And if she loses this job . . . I think back to how things were only a few weeks ago—and about the fact that she's already barricaded herself in a meat locker.

"It's okay, Mom," I say. "I messed up, and I have to face the consequences."

Captain Thomas's eyebrow goes up, as if he might be a tiny bit impressed. "Very well. If your performance has improved by the end of the week, I'll return your apparatus to you when we arrive in Fort Lauderdale."

I nod, trying to bite back the stinging feeling in my throat. The cruise isn't even half over. How am I supposed to spend the rest of the trip without my camera? I've had it by my side practically every minute for the past couple of years, so even a few days will feel like forever. And what if I see an amazing scar or mole for Alyssa's collection and won't be able to document it?

When we leave the captain's office, Mom gives my shoulder a squeeze. "I'm so sorry, Ains. I feel like this is my fault. If I hadn't dragged you here—"

"No, it's not your fault," I tell her, and I'm sure it's not. I've been really careful about not taking pictures with Spies nearby, but someone told the captain about my camera. And the only person who was with me when I was taking pictures of passengers was Ian. I should have known his nice guy act was too good to be true. Once a pig, always a pig.

So why do I feel so weirdly disappointed?

Chapter 13

In the morning, as the ship makes its way to San Juan, I find another note from Mom along with a brand-new sign to put over the entrance of the former Oven.

"The Cool Spot?" Katy reads over my shoulder. "Is that really better than the Hot Spot?"

"I don't know," I admit, "but at least people won't be trying to check their email there anymore. Plus, it doesn't sound like they'll burn up alive the minute they go inside."

"True," Katy says, but I can tell she's not sold.

"Mom says she thinks it'll 'attract the young folks.'"

"Do *you* think it'll work?" Katy asks.

"No, but I can't tell her that. She'll . . ." What can I say? That Mom might crumble if I don't wave my pom-poms at all her ideas? That's not exactly something I can admit to a girl I've only known for a few days, especially when Mom is also kind of her boss. So instead, I shrug and say, "It's worth a shot, right?"

"Do you need help putting up the sign?" Katy says.

"Thanks, but that's okay." I'm sure I'll figure it out.

"Don't forget, you're judging the cannonball contest today." She giggles. "Do you think I should wear lipstick to the gym? Will that make it too obvious that I'm only there to talk to Smith?"

"I doubt he'll notice," I say, which Katy seems to take as an encouragement to cover her entire face with makeup. She looks great, though, and I kind of wish she were my older sister or something. Then maybe I'd actually know how to put on mascara. If Smith weren't so full of himself, he actually might notice her. "Good luck," I tell her before heading out for the day.

A few minutes later, I'm standing on tiptoe on a wobbly barstool over the entrance of the lounge, trying to get the tape on the back of the sign to stick before I topple over. Maybe I should have accepted Katy's offer to help, but it's too late now. At least Ian the Traitor doesn't waltz by and try to catch me in his arms or something.

Finally, I manage to get the sign up without injuring myself. Then I go replace some of my pathetic paper palm trees with snowflakes. Lame, yes, but it's better than bare walls.

When I get to the activity center, I'm shocked to see there are probably twice as many kids as yesterday. Word must really be spreading that the towel-folding class is a chance for kids to go hog wild. Great.

"What are we making today?" Nathan asks, sounding oddly eager.

"Um . . . what would you like to make?" I haven't even had a second to look through the towel-folding book again. Not that it matters anyway, since the kids will probably shoot down whatever I come up with.

He furrows his brow, his glasses sliding down his nose. "You don't know what we're doing today, do you?"

He doesn't wait for my pathetic response. Instead, his face brightens. "Can I choose?"

He looks so excited that I sigh and hold out the towel-folding book. "Fine. But pick something easy."

"No problem!" He grabs the book from me, sprawls on the floor, and starts flipping through.

Huh. Maybe I should've had him help me before. It's the perfect solution.

"Listen up, everyone!" I call. "Nathan is going to be showing you how to make the animals today. I'll be here if anyone needs help." Help messing up their towel animals, that is.

"Let's make elephants!" Nathan announces, holding up the book so the kids can see the picture.

I expect the kids to revolt again, but miraculously, everyone seems into it. The directions say that we're supposed to use one bath towel and one hand towel, but the cart has small towels—pink, of course—so I give everyone two of those and hope it doesn't make too much of a difference.

Nathan talks everyone through what they're supposed to do, demonstrating with his own towel creation. His elephant has a giant head compared to the rest of its body, probably because of the wrong-sized towels, but no one seems to notice. I relax a little. Things are actually under control.

And then I hear someone crying. I turn to discover that Sophia has managed to wind the two towels around her head so that she can't see.

"I'm scared of the dark!" she shrieks.

I just manage to wrestle the towels away from her eyes when Jorman throws his elephant down in frustration and declares, "It's not working. And I don't want to make a girl elephant anyway!"

Next to him, a little boy starts crying because his elephant "looks stupid." Meanwhile, a couple of kids in the corner have given up on elephants and are holding up their towels so that a girl can run through them like a bull. It only takes her a second to crash into a wall.

Amid the chaos, Nathan is running around yelling, "No, you have to fold it this way! You call that a roll? What are you, a baby?"

I stand there totally helpless for a second. I'm too exhausted to do anything. Why bother getting the kids under control when they're going to walk all over me anyway?

"Can we have a food fight today?" the orange-haired boy from yesterday asks. "I brought fruit salad." He grins as he pulls pieces of lint-covered melon out of his pockets. Ick.

"I don't think so," I say as Sophia wraps herself around my leg for some reason. "Too messy."

"But you said we could do anything!" the orange-haired boy says. "Whatever we wanted!"

"Food fight!" some of the other kids yell, and soon the whole group is chanting "Food fight! Food fight!" I'm tempted to cover my ears and curl up in the corner.

As if things couldn't get worse, at that moment, the door swings open and Ian the Pig waltzes in.

"Looks like you could use some help," he says, acting as if he didn't totally rat me out to the captain.

I'm about to shoot him down when I notice that my ankle feels oddly . . . wet. When I look down, I find two wide eyes staring up at me.

"I had an accident," Sophia whispers, still wrapped around my leg.

I glance back at Ian and realize he's not by the doorway anymore. Instead, he's in the middle of the room, tossing towels up into the air and then catching them. He's totally ignoring the kids as if he always stands around juggling for fun. After a second, the screams begin to die down as the kids start to pay attention to what he's doing.

"Wow, you're pretty good," Nathan says.

Ian only shrugs and keeps juggling, pretending to almost drop something and then doing a dramatic dive to catch it. The kids shriek with laughter.

Seeing my chance, I grab Sophia's hand and lead her to the bathroom. When she's all cleaned up (and I've scrubbed at my ankle until the skin is nearly raw), we head back into the activity room to find the others are each holding two small juggling balls, trying to mimic Ian's movements. Where on earth did he even find those?

Sophia runs off to join the group, and I stand off to the side, quietly watching the kids having fun. Despite myself, I can't help admiring how easily Ian deals with them. Instead of asking them to do things, he simply shows them and assumes they'll follow his lead. I guess his piggish personality actually works in his favor in this case.

Once the kids have tired themselves out with the juggling, Ian says, "Now let's make some towel animals that you can show off to your parents." He hands the reins back over to me, and the kids are suddenly all ears.

"After we make the elephants, you guys can name them," I say, trying hard to sound confident. "So, um, grab your towels and let's start folding."

A few minutes later, we have a few pretty decent elephants made and one King of the Elephants, courtesy of Nathan, that could probably go in a museum. I send the kids off to name their animals, and then I start cleaning up the room. As I push the towel cart back into place, I find Ian standing only inches from me. He's smiling for some reason, revealing a couple of dimples I hadn't noticed before. Ugh. His stupid dimples that got my camera taken away.

I realize that Ian isn't only lurking over me, but he also seems to be sniffing the air around me.

"What?" I say, despite the fact that I'm tempted to give him the silent treatment.

"You smell like pee," he says with a laugh.

My cheeks ignite as I glance down at my ankle. How can there still be pee on it after all that scrubbing?

"But I'm willing to overlook that," Ian goes on, "if you want to go run lines again."

"Are you kidding me? After what you did?"

He actually takes a surprised step back. "What are you talking about? A deal's a deal. I help you and you help me, remember?"

I roll my eyes. "I'm pretty sure you broke that deal."

"What are—?"

"Don't bother denying it. I know it was you. Just when I was starting to think you weren't a total pig, you proved me wrong."

Before he can try to protest again, parents start bustling in to collect their kids, and soon the room is empty. I expect to find Piggy Ian lurking in the corner, waiting for the perfect moment to tell me that my fly is down or something, but he's gone too.

Good riddance.

Chapter 14

"Oh good, our judge is here!" Aussie Andy says when I arrive at the pool at noon dressed as Briar Rose, my wig itching as if it's full of fire ants in the humidity. "Where's Katy?" he whispers to me so the dozens of little kids nearby can't hear.

"She, uh, wasn't feeling that great," I say. Gah. I hate that I have to lie, but I can't exactly say that she's at the gym trying to woo Smith with her bicep curls!

"Well, I'm glad you could join us."

I sit down in the judge's chair and shove my enormous dress down around me while practicing my big, theatrical wave and hoping I don't sweat to death before the contest is over.

Aussie Andy turns back to the crowd and says into the mic, "Who's ready for the Belly Flop Like an Ogre Competition?"

Wait. The what?

"I thought this was a cannonball contest," I say.

Aussie Andy just laughs and tells the contestants to get into position. How am I supposed to judge how an ogre would flop into a pool? Can ogres even swim?

But the kids are all looking at me eagerly, so I paste my standard "everything is awesome" smile on my face and say in what I hope is a princess voice, "I look forward to seeing what you ogres have in store for me!"

A few of the kids roar back at me, and I can't help laughing. Maybe this is going to be more fun than I thought.

Aussie Andy hands me some cards that are numbered one through five and whispers, "Go easy on 'em." The kids line up, and when Aussie Andy gives them the go-ahead, they start flopping into the pool one by one.

The first boy starts to flop but winds up doing a half cannonball instead. I realize that all eyes are suddenly on me. Oh, right. I'm supposed to actually judge.

I think for a second and then hold up a three. The crowd boos. Huh. I guess when Aussie Andy said to go easy on the kids, he meant *really* easy.

Up next is a boy who must be a professional diver because he does the most graceful swan dive off the diving board that I've ever seen. I want to give him a five because he's so good, but since there was absolutely nothing ogre-ish about his dive, I give it a four. The crowd boos again. Wow, I really can't get this right.

A few belly floppers later, the crowd officially hates me. I've given pretty much everyone a four because I'm afraid to give higher or lower scores.

"This is boring!" someone yells.

Finally, a girl gets up on the diving board. She looks a lot older than the other contestants, and I actually wonder if she might be my age. No one seems to care, though, because she's putting on a great show.

She's totally in character, scratching her armpits like a monkey and grunting. Then she hurls herself off the board and hits the water with a deafening smack. The crowd gasps as she shoots out of the pool with blood dripping from her nose.

"Are you all right, honey?" Aussie Andy calls to her, but she doesn't pay attention to him because she's crying. She looks okay, but the force of hitting the water must have given her a bloody nose.

No one's paying attention to me anymore, but I weakly hold up a five anyway.

"And that's our last contestant!" Aussie Andy yells, clearly trying to get things back on track. "And I think we have a winner." He points to the girl who's still sobbing into a towel while her mom hugs her tight. "Congrats, sweetheart! You win a free smoothie at the Oven! Er, I mean, the Hot—no, the *Cool* Spot!"

I hold back a laugh. The smoothies at the Cool Spot are free—a lot of the food and drinks on the ship are—but making it sound like a special prize is a great way to get some more people to go there. Aussie Andy really is a pro.

To my surprise, the girl starts crying even harder. "I'm lactose intolerant!"

"And," Aussie Andy chimes in, "you also get your picture taken with a princess."

The girl looks up at me and grimaces. "With her?"

"If you'd like," Aussie Andy says. "Or with one of the other princesses on board. Your choice."

"Wait!" someone calls. "She's not a princess!" I turn to see Jorman pointing at me. "She folds towels!"

"Maybe she's Cinderella," one of the girls says.

"She doesn't even know who Cinderella is," a girl in a sparkly pink bathing suit answers. Sure enough, it's one of the mini Barbies from the first day of the cruise.

"My Edwina won a prize," the winner's mother says. "She deserves a prize she actually *wants*!"

Aussie Andy and I exchange looks. I bet if Katy were here, she'd be able to smooth things over with that bubbly charm of hers. Too bad she's off drooling over Smith. Wait . . .

"Hey," I say to Edwina, "what about a date with Prince Handsome?"

She looks at me, her tears suddenly gone. "You mean the prince from the show? He's so cute!" Her expression turns dreamy, and even her mom looks a little dazed at the thought of Smith. Ick.

"Yeah, if you want, you can go on a special date with him." I have no idea how I'll get Smith to agree to this plan, but at least the girl isn't sobbing anymore. "With your mom, of course."

Edwina's mom looks like she might burst from happiness. "Thank you so much!" she gushes. "That would be wonderful."

Her daughter finally smiles. "This is going to be awesome," she declares.

Phew.

"And that's the end of the contest!" Aussie Andy says, clearly trying to wrap up the event before anything else goes wrong. "Thanks for joining in the fun. We'll be doing fairy tale trivia in an hour at the John and the Celery Stalk Lounge."

I'm tempted to tear off my itchy wig as I retreat from the pool, but I tell myself to keep it together until I'm back in my room. I don't want to give the captain any more ammo to use against me. So I stagger along through the narrow corridors, my enormous dress brushing against the walls on either side of me. On my way, I stop at the photo kiosk to see how things are going.

Mitch! is sprawled on the floor, trying to get some little kids to pose in front of an ugly backdrop of a castle while the youngest one gnaws on a foam prop tower.

When they're all done, Mitch! scrambles to his feet and looks right at me. "Hey, you're the one who gave me that advice about getting down on the ground when I'm taking pictures of little kids, right?"

"Yup, that was me." It's a miracle he recognized me in my princess getup.

"Great tip. I've sold a bunch more pictures thanks to you. How did you know to do that?"

"I like photography," I tell him. "I want to be a wildlife photographer when I get older. You know, the people who go into jungles and take pictures of rare animals." I laugh. "The closest I've come is taking pictures of squirrels in my backyard, but I keep hoping we'll at least see a whale while we're out here."

"How old are you?" he says.

"Thirteen," I say. Then I silently add "almost" so it's not a lie.

"Wow. And you work here?"

"My mom's the cruise director, so they made an exception for me. Actually, my mom said people have been having problems with their photos," I say slowly, trying not to offend him.

"Yeah, they keep complaining, saying I don't know what I'm doing." He shrugs. "You know how people are with family photos. They want everything to be perfect."

"Maybe I could help?" I say.

"You? You're just a kid."

"Oh, as an assistant or a junior photographer in training or something. It would be such good experience!" I paste on my brightest, most hopeful smile. Mom can't accuse me of meddling if I convince her that I'm helping at the kiosk to get some professional experience under my belt.

"Sure, why not?" Mitch! says. "How about you start now?"

"Now? But I have to go change." Not only is my wig driving me crazy, but my dress is so thick that I can feel sweat dripping down my back.

"No, that's okay. If a kid wants a picture with a princess, we'll throw you in the shot. It'll be great."

I sigh. "Great."

And just like that, I have yet another job on the cruise. At this rate, I'll be running the whole ship by myself by the end of the summer.

Chapter 15

After I help Mitch! with photos for half an hour—which basically consists of me watching him flirt with all the dads—he turns to me and says, "I really have to go to the bathroom. Can you hold down the fort for a minute? You don't have to do a thing except keep things calm until I get back."

"Sure."

As he disappears, the people in line start grumbling, and the kids in front of the backdrop start fighting over who gets to be next to the fake deer that's part of the scenery. The mom asks me, "Any chance you have a second deer?"

"Sorry," I say, and the youngest kid lets out a shriek. "But . . . we have some swords. Would you guys rather be knights in a castle?" That backdrop, at least, won't clash with what the kids are wearing.

Their eyes light up. "Yeah!"

I know I should wait for Mitch! to come back, but I'm afraid the other people in line will start rioting, and the last thing we want is word getting back to the captain that there are even more problems at the photo kiosk. So I quickly change out the backdrop, push the deer off to the side, and hand out some foam swords.

"Now, pose!" I say, setting up behind the camera.

"You're taking the pictures?" the dad asks, clearly skeptical.

"Just until Mitch! gets back. To test the lights and stuff."

That seems to reassure them because they start listening to me. I have them shift around a little to get the best lighting, and then I start snapping pictures. After a few shots, a notification on the camera asks if I want to make the pictures "normal resolution" to fit more on the memory card. Since I want to make sure not to run out of room, I select "okay" and keep snapping.

By the time Mitch! comes back, I have at least a couple shots I can use.

"Whoa," he says. "Looks like you went ahead without me."

"Sorry," I say. "I got inspired."

"These look great!" the mom says, peering over my shoulder at the image display. "I know they were just test shots, but I don't think we need to do any more. Thanks!"

"Nice job, kid," Mitch! says when they're gone. "I think that's the happiest customer we've had this whole cruise."

I can't help giving myself a little pat on the back for that one. Then I look at the long line of passengers still waiting to get their pictures taken, and I get back to work.

Before the show that night, I peek into the teen lounge—aka the Cool Spot—to see how things are going. This time, it's full of old people. Not a single teenager in sight.

"This place is hotter than Hades!" an ancient-looking woman is saying.

"They could at least have some decent drinks," an old man grumbles. "They're trying to pawn off those green smoothies on us. What's kale anyway? Some kind of seaweed? I don't want seaweed in my dentures."

Yikes.

"Aren't you supposed to be getting into costume right now?" one of the Spies hisses in my ear.

I mean, seriously, do they have everyone's schedule memorized?

I realize this is the same woman I saw standing guard here last time. Her name tag says her name is Wanda. "You spend a lot of time in this place," I say. "Any idea why it's usually so empty?"

"Atmosphere," she says immediately, as if she's been waiting for someone to ask her opinion. "A place needs atmosphere."

"What did you have in mind?"

Wanda shrugs. "It's a ship, right? So maybe some fish, some dolphins, that kind of thing."

"Like pictures of them on the walls?"

"No, real ones, swimming in tanks. You know. Fun stuff. Kids like fun. Maybe a shark."

I blink at her. "You want a *shark* on board the ship?"

"It would draw a crowd, right?"

"That's true . . . But how would you tie that into the fairy tale theme?"

"Sharks can't be in fairy tales?" Wanda barks. "Who says they're not?"

"I—I don't know. I guess they could be, even if they're never mentioned." I'm suddenly afraid she might gobble me up, shark-style. "They could be . . . in the background or something. Like maybe in *Briar Rose*, there's a shark swimming around in the moat while she's sleeping inside the castle for a hundred years."

"Exactly. See? Now you're thinking. You wanted

my advice. There it is. All right, it's three minutes past the time when you were supposed to be at the theater. Do you want me to report you?"

"No!" I say, already shuffling away.

When I get to the theater, the first person I see is Neil. He's sitting in the front row with his Moleskine notebook again, probably writing more vocabulary words.

"Any good words today?" I find myself asking. Ugh. Couldn't I have come up with something better than that?

He looks up from his notebook and gives me that sparkling smile of his. "Not really. Do you know what"—he glances down—"*topiary* is?"

"Sure, it's when you trim bushes and shrubs and stuff to look like animals."

"You're making that up!" he says with a laugh.

"No! I swear it's a thing."

"If you say so," he says, giving my foot a playful tap with his toe. My shoe just about lights on fire. Oh my gosh. Is he flirting with me? "By the way, your hair looks nice today."

I self-consciously touch my ponytail. "Thanks. I wear it like this all the time, but . . . thanks."

"So listen," Neil says. "I was wondering . . ."

Oh my gosh. It's finally happening!

"If you'd want to—"

He's finally asking me out on a date!

"Ainsley!" My mom's voice echoes across the stage. "Ainsley, is that you?"

Groan. Can't I have a single conversation with Neil that lasts more than thirty seconds?

Neil jumps to his feet. "Hey, Lydia," he says, giving her a bright grin. "You look great today."

"Oh, thank you," Mom says, tucking her hair behind her ear. "By the way, Neil, would you mind helping with theater cleanup after the show tonight? We're a little shorthanded."

Neil's smile stiffens a little, but he nods. "Sure thing!" Then he tucks his notebook under his arm and heads backstage. I expect him to glance back over his shoulder at me, maybe give me a sad little smile, but he doesn't. Maybe he's as frustrated about our interrupted conversation as I am.

Mom turns to me and sighs. "Bad news about the Cool Spot—"

"I know. I stopped by there earlier. Maybe I can help you come up with some ideas for how to make it better?"

Mom shakes her head. "I'm sure I can figure it out. I used to be great at this kind of thing."

"Well . . . if you want some help, I'm here."

"Thanks, Ains. I appreciate it. Now you'd better go get ready for the show. Break a leg!"

I'm hoping to talk to Neil again in the dressing room, but he's busy goofing around with some of the other dwarves. Instead, I head over to get my costume and find Smith standing in front of the mirror, seemingly admiring his own reflection. I must have fairy tales on the brain because I can't help imagining him asking the mirror who's the "hottest of them all."

"Hey," I say. Time to convince him to go on a fake date with Edwina and her mom.

"Back for more acting tips?" He strikes what I think is supposed to be a dramatic pose, but he looks more ice sculpture than Hamlet.

"Um, no." I'm tempted to smack him away like a fly. "I wanted to talk to you, though."

"Yeah?" Then he goes back to staring at his own reflection, his eyes practically bugging out of his head. "Why is this so hard?" he says with a groan.

"What is?"

"I'm trying to raise one of my eyebrows. I'll let you in on a little secret: The key to good acting is being able to lift your eyebrows one at a time."

"I would think the secret to acting would be saying your lines like you mean them. And moving your arms around."

Smith shakes his head. "No, trust me, all the greats have really expressive eyebrows. Maybe I could tape one of them up, and it'll eventually learn to do it on its own. Can you do me a favor and find some tape?"

I sigh. "Sure. But you have to do a favor for me too. I need you to go on a date with a girl and her mom." Then I explain about the belly flop contest. "You'll have to talk to Aussie Andy about setting it up."

I expect him to say something gross or conceited again—or to flat-out refuse to do it—but he only shrugs and says, "Okay. I'll make sure they have a good time."

"Really?"

"Yeah, why not? I always love meeting fans," he says, as if he's been a fake prince for years instead of only a couple of days.

"Well . . . thanks." That was easier than I thought. "How was working out at the gym today, by the way?" I not-so-subtly ask.

"Fine, why?"

"No reason. I think my roommate was going to be there too. You know Katy? She's the Mermaid Princess."

"The one who always talks about her dog? I think she's got a thing for me."

"Sh-she does? How can you tell?"

Smith gives me a gleaming smile. "Because they all do."

Gross. As if every girl is pining after him.

I rifle around the dressing room until I find a roll of masking tape in someone's makeup kit. As I go to hand it to Smith, I spot Piggy Ian walking into the room. When he sees me, he gives me an uncertain wave. I quickly turn away. Somehow, the roll of tape shoots out of my hand and smacks Smith on the side of the head.

"Ow!" Smith yells. Then he lets out a whoop of joy. "I think I got it! Ashley, look!"

As far as I can tell, his eyebrows look exactly the same as they did before, but I give him a thumbs-up and say, "Good job." Then I waltz past Piggy Ian without a word.

I'm determined to get onstage on my own before the show, but when the curtain is about to open, I'm frozen in the wings again. My stupid legs won't move no matter what I do, and my breath is making a weird rattling sound in my chest.

"Places!"

This is it. I won't be able to get out onstage, and it'll ruin the show, and the captain will chew me out for sure. But the worst part is imagining the look of disappointment on Mom's face when she realizes I've totally let her down.

"Come on," someone whispers in my ear. It's Ian.

"No," I whisper. "I don't want help from someone like you."

"What do you mean 'someone like—?'"

"Places!" Stefan calls again.

I still can't move, and suddenly things start spinning around me. Oh no. I can't pass out again! And definitely not in the wings!

Before I can object, Ian grabs my elbow and practically carries me out onstage and deposits me on the mattress. Then he disappears without a word. I want to hate him—how dare he help me when I'm so furious at him?—but I'm too freaked out to do anything but lie on the mattress and try not to black out.

Chapter 16

In the morning, I'm surprised to discover there's no note from Mom or new sign outside my door. I doubt she's given up, but maybe this means she's more stuck than she was letting on. I'll have to start doubling up on the brainstorming, in case she actually lets me help her.

"How was talking to Smith at the gym yesterday?" I ask Katy as we head off to work after breakfast. She was out late last night with the other mermaids again, so I didn't get the scoop. She keeps inviting me to hang out with the other girls, but I'm barely getting enough sleep as it is.

Katy sighs and starts telling me about how she got nervous and started doing an imitation of her dog for him. "And Smith said, 'Were you barking, or is that what your voice sounds like?' and I was mortified!" She shakes her head. "I wish I could stop making such a fool out of myself every time I'm around him. So far, he's only noticed me for the wrong reasons!"

Oh boy. I can certainly relate to that. One of these days, maybe I'll actually have a conversation with Neil about something other than vocabulary words.

"But the second he's around," Katy goes on, "all I do is talk about Snoopy." As she talks, her voice gets louder and louder, until passengers are staring at her as we pass by. I guess it must be pretty weird to hear the Mermaid Princess talking about a dog.

Suddenly, I spot Curt nearby. The Spies really have a sixth sense about this kind of stuff, don't they? "Katy," I say softly, "you might want to—"

But it's too late.

"Katherine Abrams!" Curt barks. "Can I see you for a minute?"

He pulls her over to a corner and, I assume, starts lecturing her about staying in character, all while keeping a bright smile on his face. To anyone else, it would look as if they're having a friendly chat, except for the stunned look on her face. Clearly, she had no idea she was doing anything wrong. I feel bad for her, and even worse that I can't stick around to make sure she's okay because I have to go get ready for my class.

I hurry off into the bowels of the ship and venture into the laundry cavern to find Adelina among the towel mountains and bedsheet cliffs. People are sorting through the stacks, throwing things into enormous washing machines or pulling them out of driers. It's loud and hot and chaotic. I suddenly have a whole new appreciation for my jobs.

Adelina and a stooped older woman are pressing shirts on the other end of the room. When I get closer, I can't help overhearing their conversation.

"Poor man," Adelina is saying, her Rs trilling off her tongue. "He was so different before the accident.

When I worked on this ship with the yarn people, he was always smiling. And now . . .”

“His hand is gone and so is his smile,” the other woman says.

They have to mean Captain Thomas, don't they? But the idea that he could have ever been anything but his surly self seems impossible. And he was the captain here when the ship was still a knitting cruise? I had thought all the crew was totally new.

“Oh, Ainsley,” Adelina says, finally noticing me. “How are you?” I'm surprised she remembers my name, but maybe if you call the captain “Hook” in front of a bunch of people, you kind of stick in their memories.

“Um, okay. I was wondering if I could get some bigger towels.” I tell her about yesterday's towel-folding fiasco. I'm tempted to ask her for non-pink towels, but I don't want to press my luck.

“Of course,” she says. “This way.” She leads me down a narrow hallway into a room full of perfectly stacked towels and linens. Nearly half of them are accidental-pink. “Help yourself.”

"Thanks." I can't help adding, "So you've known Captain Thomas a long time? Sorry, I overheard your conversation."

"Oh yes," she says. "Over ten years. A lot has changed since he was with the knitters."

"You said there was an accident. What happened?" I ask.

"A boating trip." She looks around, as if making sure it's okay to tell me more. Then she continues in a soft voice. "He was on the water with friends, and no one was paying attention to the weather. Suddenly, a storm came and the boat capsized. Everyone was rescued, but the poor captain lost his arm. After that, he was never the same. I think he blames himself for not being more cautious. Now that he runs an entire ship, it seems all he thinks about is being careful." Adelina shakes her head sadly. "I must get back to work." Then she shoos me away before I can ask any more questions.

For once, I get to the towel-folding class early. I'm surprised to find Nathan there by himself.

"My parents and sister are going on a snorkeling excursion today," he explains, "so they left me with some old lady for the day, but she wanted to go to the casino, so she brought me here early."

"No snorkeling for you?" I ask Nathan. I would have figured he'd be the first one off the ship, ready to tell all the locals what they were doing wrong.

He shrugs. "I'm not allowed to be out in the sun. It makes me break out in hives."

"Wow." I guess that explains the long sleeves and hat he always wears. No wonder he's so into origami and other indoor stuff. "Why did your parents take you on a Caribbean cruise?" I can't help asking. "It's a lot of time in the sun."

He doesn't look up from the origami book he's reading. "Because my sister really wanted to go on a Disney cruise for her birthday, but we couldn't afford it, so this was the next best thing. Wait, you know her. Edwina, the one who won the belly flop contest. She told me all about it after."

"She's your sister?" I realize the two of them kind of look alike, and they certainly both have the perfectionist thing down.

"Yup," he says. "My parents never tell her no. Last year, we all went to Six Flags for my birthday, even though I was too small to go on any of the rides. Guess whose idea that was? I wanted to go to this place where you can look at dinosaur bones and stuff, but my sister said it was too boring."

The poor kid. "Did you tell your parents how you feel?"

"What's the point? She'll throw a fit, and they'll do whatever she wants. They tell me they'll make it up to me next time, and Dad always says I'm a trooper, but I doubt we'll ever get to go." He glares at me. "Why are you smiling?"

"Nothing, sorry. It's just . . . my mom calls me her little trooper too. I think our parents would get along."

He shrugs. "At least you get to do stuff you want to do," he says.

This time I have to laugh. "Trust me. You're not the only one who's stuck here. But we'll make the best of it, okay?"

Nathan shrugs, but at least he doesn't look so glum anymore.

The door opens, and a bunch of other kids come rushing in. There aren't as many as yesterday, but I'm still surrounded.

"Are we juggling again?" Jorman asks.

"Nope, we're making towel lions today!" I announce. Not only do I know nothing about juggling, but I'm definitely not following Piggy Ian's lead.

The kids stare at me, clearly unimpressed.

"Or . . . towel monkeys!"

Nothing.

"Whales?"

Someone behind me starts whimpering, and I know I have to think fast. I can't let the class go totally chaotic again.

"Okay, forget towels. How about . . ." My brain churns, scrounging for an idea. "You want to learn how to walk like a prince or a princess?" It's a fairy tale cruise, after all. They should want to do that kind of stuff, right?

"I don't want to be a prince," Jorman says. "Princes are for girls."

"And for babies," Nathan adds.

"What about a knight?" I say.

That seems to get a slightly better reaction.

"I like princesses," Sophia tells me, "but only if they sing. Can we sing while we're walking?"

"Um, sure."

"What about space aliens?" another girl asks. "Can we learn to walk like them?"

"Why not?"

Before they change their minds, I usher the kids into the corner and have them make a couple of lines. Then I do my best to demonstrate how a knight walks.

"You're doing it wrong," Nathan informs me. "You have to pretend like you're wearing really heavy armor." Then he does a knight walk that would make Sir Lancelot proud.

"Okay, everyone do what Nathan is doing!" I call out, and this time, having the kids follow his lead actually pays off. That's when I get an idea.

"Sophia," I say after everyone's tried a knight walk. "Show us how a singing princess walks."

She smiles and struts around the room, belting Disney songs at the top of her lungs. The kids start mimicking her, even the boys, and pretty soon, everyone's giggling.

"Your turn," I say, pointing to the girl who asked about the aliens. "How do little green men walk?"

"On their toes!" she says. "And they're trying to suck people's brains out!" She starts tiptoeing around the room, making little sucking sounds and wiggling her fingers. Soon, everyone in the room, including me, is following her lead.

"This is fun!" Jorman says, and my face hurts from smiling so much.

We keep going like this for a few minutes, coming up with weirder and weirder creatures to imitate. When we're all clucking and pretending to be four-legged chickens, the door swings open. I expect it to be one of the parents, but it's not. It's much worse.

"What's going on in here?" Captain Thomas asks. This time he has a pair of binoculars tucked under his arm. "I could hear you all the way from my office."

The room goes silent. The kids might have never seen the captain before, but it's obvious that they're instantly cowed by him. They all stare at the compass spinning inside his hook hand.

"S-sorry if we were too loud," I stammer. "We were—"

"Not folding towels," the captain observes.

"Walking like chickens!" Sophia cries. She might be scared of a lot of things, but clearly the captain doesn't intimidate her. "And like aliens and puppets and monkeys and dandelions!"

Captain Thomas looks at her for a second. Then he leans down, and I'm afraid he's going to yell at her to go swab the deck. Instead, he smiles and says in a surprisingly gentle voice, "And how does a dandelion walk?"

She grins back at him. "Like this!" she says. Then she starts marching around the room, singing Disney songs at the top of her lungs again.

Oh no. Disney in any form is *so* not allowed on this ship. I expect the captain's head to explode, but instead, he simply watches her with an amused glint in his eyes. Huh. I guess if the passengers are the ones breaking the rules, it doesn't matter.

"Very good," the captain tells her. Then he turns to Jorman. "And what about you? What was your favorite walk?"

Jorman thinks for a second and then says, "A pirate!" and starts marching around.

My mouth falls open. "Pirate" was not one of our walks. I think he just called Captain Thomas a pirate to his face! That's almost as bad as calling him Captain Hook.

I'm sure Captain Thomas is going to roar at him. But instead, he says, "My son loved being a pirate when he was little." Then, to my total shock, the captain puffs out his chest and announces, "This is how a pirate walks!" He starts swashbuckling around, pretending to fight off an enemy with an imaginary sword. The kids instantly start imitating him, and they're having so much fun that even I'm inspired to get in a few sword jabs.

I can't believe it. Who knew there was an actual human under the captain's stiff uniform and terrifying glare?

Finally, when the kids are falling over themselves laughing, the captain hands the reins over to Nathan—who immediately starts doing a caveman walk—and then waves me over to the corner.

"Miss Parker," the captain says, his face suddenly stern again. "Let me remind you that this is a *towel-folding* class."

I gulp as I watch the kids still lumbering around after Nathan, laughing and giggling. They might be having fun, but the captain is right. "Y-yes, sir. I know, sir. I'll make sure we do what we're supposed to from now on."

"One more misstep and . . ." He doesn't need to

finish. We both know what happens to employees who break the rules on this ship. The captain turns and gives the kids a little salute. "Carry on, everyone!"

The kids watch him retreat and then start shrieking with excitement.

"What are we doing now?" Sophia asks.

"Let's walk like ship captains!" Nathan cries. And before I can stop them, all the kids are running around the room doing their best impressions of Captain Thomas. This time, I don't join in.

Chapter 17

I find Mom waiting for me outside the Fairy Fun Zone after class, and for a second I'm terrified that she's here because the captain told her how bad I've been at my job. But she doesn't look upset, only thoughtful.

"What's going on?" I ask.

"I'm just trying to figure out what to do about the teen nightclub," she says.

"It's too bad no one goes there. Their smoothies are awesome," I say. "And Matthieu puts so much time into making them. Katy says you can practically taste the love!"

Mom nods slowly. "Maybe we can highlight the smoothies somehow."

"What about something like the 'Smoothie Lounge'?" I ask. "At least then people might go there for the drinks."

"Maybe . . ." I can tell she's not convinced. Suddenly, her face lights up. "I know! What about 'Blended with Love'?"

I try not to groan. It's so cheesy, but Mom is clearly excited about the idea. "Why not?" I say weakly. I can put little hearts up around the place and play romantic music or something. That might give it a little more atmosphere, at least.

"Great!" Mom says. "I'll send along a new sign for you to put up this afternoon." She starts scurrying away. "Oh, wait!" she calls, coming to a stop. "I almost forgot. Any chance you could do me a favor?"

Why does she even bother asking?

"Gemma is feeling under the weather and won't be able to make an appearance by the pool after lunch today. Any chance you could do it? We really need a princess there. It'll only be for a couple of hours."

"Um, I'd have to rush over from helping at the photo kiosk," I say. "And it won't give me much time to get ready for dinner duty—"

"So you'll be able to fit it in?" She looks so hopeful that all I can do is nod. "You're the best, Ains!" she says. Then she gives my arm a squeeze and hurries away.

When I rush to the pool in my princess costume that afternoon, I'm relieved to see Katy there.

"Ainsley!" she says. "What are you doing here?"

"Gemma's sick, so my mom asked me to take over."

"Couldn't one of the other princesses do it?" she asks, reaching out to straighten my wig. "You look like you could use a break."

I shrug. "It's fine. Only a couple of hours, right?"

"Well, I'm glad you're here. You can finally meet some of the other sea creatures!"

Katy introduces me to a girl named Mai who's playing a siren and another one named Elaine who's playing a selkie, although I wouldn't know their roles based on their costumes. They all just look a little seaweedy.

I get in place beside them, ready to start waving and posing for pictures with kids, as Katy chatters on and on. I realize that since Mai's first language isn't English—she's from Thailand—and Elaine seems really shy, they both let Katy talk and talk. No wonder she loves spending so much time with them.

Unfortunately, I'm afraid her talking is going to get us into trouble, especially when she cries, "Oh, Ainsley! I forgot to tell you that Smith smiled at me at breakfast!"

A little girl with long pigtails glares up at me. "Aren't you Sleeping Beauty?"

"I'm Briar Rose, Sleeping Beauty's cousin!" I don't have the energy to explain about the different versions of fairy tales.

"Then why did she call you Ainsley?" the girl asks.

"Um, it's my nickname," I say through my fake smile. "Do you want your picture taken with me?"

"No, thanks," she says. "I'm going to go find a real princess."

"Katy," I say in a whisper, "you have to stay in character, remember?"

She rolls her eyes. "Gosh, Ainsley. You sound like Curt. He's such a stickler for everything."

"Maybe he's a stickler because he doesn't want to get fired," I can't help saying.

"No one's getting fired," Katy says. "They just like to make a big stink out of things around here. Besides, you bend the rules all the time. Isn't that what got your camera taken away?"

"That's different! I'm trying to help people. You're just babbling because you can't stop yourself, even when you're supposed to be in character."

Her mouth falls open. "Babbling? I'm not babbling! Am I babbling?" she asks the other girls. They give meek shrugs, clearly wanting to stay out of it. And, unlike us, they're actually focusing on their jobs. "Anyway, you're not helping your mom. You're just making things worse."

"What are you talking about?"

"Come on, Ainsley. Who's the grown-up in that relationship? If you stopped helping your mom for once, maybe she'd figure things out on her own."

"You don't know anything about our relationship!" I cry. All the icky feelings that have been brewing inside me are suddenly fighting to get out. "Just because you spill your life story to me all the time doesn't mean I have to do the same."

"Well, don't worry," Katy says, "because that's the last time I tell you anything!" Then she turns and starts slithering away as fast as her fish tail can take her.

"Katy, wait!" I yell, hurrying after her. "You can't leave. You're on duty!"

She stops, as if she's realized I'm right, but when she turns back to me, the end of her tail wraps around her feet. She takes one step forward and—*whoosh!*—tumbles through the air and into the kiddie pool.

Kids scream with laughter as a mermaid belly flops on top of them. To them, it must seem like part of her act. Meanwhile, Katy thrashes in the water, trying to right herself, but her tail seems to be pulling her down.

"Stand up!" I yell, rushing to the side of the pool. "Katy, the water's shallow! Just stand up!" But she can't hear me because her head keeps sinking underwater.

"Someone help!" I scream as I try to dash into the pool to help her, but my enormous dress gets tangled around my legs, and I only wind up falling over. "Please help!"

No one's listening to my pathetic pleas. The pool is so loud that people are still laughing and swimming as if nothing's wrong, and I don't see a lifeguard anywhere.

Just when I'm about to tear off my dress and jump in the water, someone barrels past me and plunges into the pool. Then all I see are flailing arms and legs and fins, until finally someone pulls a very wet but very much alive Katy out of the pool. When the person spreads her out by the side of the pool—without her fish tail—I realize it's Ian!

"Are you okay?" he yells. "Can you breathe?"

Katy gazes up at him with hazy eyes. "I'm not sure. I think I might need CPR. Or maybe just a handsome prince?"

Ian laughs and sits back. "I think that means you're fine." Then he looks around at the crowd of parents and kids who've finally noticed that something is wrong and are standing around. One little boy is crying in terror and pointing at Katy's tail-less legs.

"Pool's open again, folks!" Ian calls. "Enjoy!"

There's a long moment of silence. And then ten seconds later, the kids are laughing and playing again. I guess when you're on vacation, you don't care if you almost see a mermaid drown.

"Ainsley," Katy says when I spread a towel over her, since she's pretty much in her underwear. "Where's my tail? They'll kill me if I lose my tail!"

Oh no. She's right. The Spies will report her for being out of costume! I run to the edge of the pool, trying to spot her tail in the crowded water. Finally, I see a group of little kids playing with it. They're throwing it at one another and shrieking to avoid it as if it's a sea monster.

When I manage to convince them to give it back to me, the tail is so heavy with water that I have to hoist it over my shoulder. No wonder Katy couldn't get out of the pool. This thing was like a hundred-pound weight around her legs.

As I finally manage to stand up, I spot Curt standing on the opposite side of the pool. His eyes say it all. We're in serious trouble.

Chapter 18

When Ian, Katy, and I get to the captain's office, we're all still sopping wet. I wish we'd at least had time to get changed, but Curt escorted us straight here.

The captain studies us for a long moment. Then he says through his teeth, "That was quite the disruption you caused at the pool."

"I'm so sorry, sir!" Katy jumps in. "I tripped and fell, and I would be dead right now if Ian hadn't saved me!"

The captain purses his lips. "I was referring to the disruption that began before you went in the water. I heard reports of an argument." His eyes laser in on me.

Oops. Of course he knows about us arguing. The whole ship probably heard us yelling at each other.

The captain lets out a long breath through his nose. "And on top of that, you interrupt people in the pool and bring children to tears! We can't have that kind of behavior from our staff. It's unacceptable."

"To be fair, we only brought one kid to tears," I can't help saying softly.

The captain's dark eyes get so round, they look like two cannons ready to fire.

"Can't you give them a break?" Ian pipes up. "The rules are in place for a reason. I get it. But they're not stealing from passengers like Douglas did. Doesn't everyone deserve a second chance?"

Whoa. Why is he standing up for us?

I expect the captain to put Ian in his place, but instead he says, "Fine. I will let this incident slide. But this is your final warning. Now get back to work." Then he waves us toward the door.

Katy shoots to her feet and dashes out of the room,

clearly trying to make a run for it in case the captain changes his mind.

"Except for you, Miss Parker," the captain adds. "I want to see you in private."

Ian gives me a look I can't quite read before he ducks through the door. Then I'm all alone with the captain, his hook gleaming at me in the light. If he starts sharpening it, I'm out of here.

"Miss Parker," he says. "Why is it that I keep hearing your name? First your camera, now this. On top of that, I'm told you don't report for your shifts on time, you're not prepared for rehearsals, and we both know how little towel folding goes on in that class of yours."

I stare down at the floor.

"So I think it's best for everyone involved if we—"

I close my eyes. Here it is. The moment when I lose this job, and Mom and I have no choice but to go home. Part of me is actually kind of relieved. Maybe coming here was a huge mistake after all.

"—put you on probation," he finishes.

My eyes snap open. "Probation? You . . . you're not firing me?"

He sighs. "Perhaps Ian was right about giving you another chance. But this is your final warning. One more mishap and you're finished. Understand?"

"Yes!" I squeak. "Thank you, sir." I jump to my feet and hurry out of his office, resisting the urge to high-five the octopus on my way out.

When I get into the hallway, I find Ian waiting for me.

"Everything okay?" he asks.

"Yeah, fine." I start to walk away, but then I pause and turn back to Ian. "Um, so I just wanted to say thank you, for saving Katy," I mumble. "And for standing up for us and everything."

"What was I going to do, watch her drown?"

That's pretty much what I'd been doing. "If I hadn't been wearing that stupid enormous dress—"

"I like that stupid enormous dress," Ian says. "It looks nice on you."

I roll my eyes. "If you like not being able to fit through doorways, maybe. Or narrow hallways."

He laughs. "Yeah, nothing narrow to worry about on this ship." He lifts his elbows and they almost graze the walls.

"Yeah, so anyway, thanks." I turn to go, but he trots after me.

"Does that mean we can run lines again? Stefan gave us some new stuff, and I really need help going through it."

"I don't think so. I haven't forgiven you yet."

"Forgiven me for what?"

"Oh, please. You know what you did."

He looks totally mystified. Wow, he really is a good actor. "Ainsley, what are you talking about? You've been acting so weird lately. I don't get it."

"Hello! Because of you, the captain took my camera away."

"Wait, what? He took your camera? Why?"

"Because you ratted me out!" I cry. "You told him I was taking pictures of the passengers, and he freaked out and said I was breaking the rules and that he'd need to confiscate my camera until we got back to Florida."

"Whoa, I swear I didn't say anything to him or to anyone else about that."

"But you're the only one who saw me taking pictures of passengers!" Why I was stupid enough to do that in front of him in the first place is beyond me. I guess that's what happens when I'm really intent on getting a good shot of something.

"Are you sure? The monitors are pretty much all over the ship. Maybe they saw you and you didn't realize it."

Could he be right? I've been so careful, but maybe not as careful as I thought. "You swear you didn't tell on me?" I ask.

"On my turtle."

I blink. "You have a turtle?"

"Yup, back home. His name is Cornelius Shellman III. He loves watermelon."

That sounds too weird to make up. "Okay, fine. I believe you."

"You really thought I'd do that to you?" he asks. "No wonder you've been giving me the serious cold shoulder. So, can we go run lines for a little while?"

"I can't. I have to go put up another sign for my mom. And no, I don't need your help."

He holds up his hands in surrender. "Suit yourself. I don't want you getting mad at me again."

"I wasn't mad at you," I say, but of course that's a total lie and we both know it.

"From now on, I think it's safer for me to stay on your good side," Ian says. "Truce?"

I'm tempted to argue that I don't have a bad side, but instead, I hold out my hand and say, "Truce."

Chapter 19

After I hurriedly change out of my damp dress, I go to the teen lounge and put up yet another sign. I also hang up some more decorations, crossing my fingers that these will actually work. Then I grab another delicious smoothie, figuring I've earned a treat.

"Heads up," I tell Matthieu. "You guys have a new name again." I explain about trying to highlight the smoothie angle and cringe when I tell him the Blended with Love idea Mom came up with.

"She is right, you know," he says. "I do make them with love." Then he blows a kiss toward the blender, which makes me crack up.

I turn to see Katy standing in the doorway, giving me an uncertain smile. All the things we said to each other by the pool flood back into my head. I don't know if I should be angry at her or beg her to forgive me. She seems not to know either, because she just stands there without moving.

Suddenly, Curt the Spy materializes next to me. "Aren't you supposed to be at the photo kiosk in a few minutes?"

"Yup!" I say, resisting the urge to stomp on his foot. "Thanks for the reminder!"

He glances at Katy who's inched a little closer to me. "I'm surprised you two still have jobs here after that scene by the pool today," he says.

"We were just talking and said some stuff we didn't really mean." At least I did.

Katy gives me a sad smile and takes another step toward me, which I guess means she feels the same way. "Sorry if it caused any trouble," she says.

Curt seems to be looking for something to criticize, but he stays quiet. Finally, he glances at me and says, "Make sure to get to the kiosk soon" before marching off.

I sigh in relief when he's gone. "I swear he's following me around the ship just so he can point out the stuff I'm doing wrong."

Katy giggles. "Maybe he has a crush on you."

"Ew!" I cry.

"What? He's kind of cute, don't you think?"

I snort. "Maybe if you're into pure evil."

She giggles again and then her face gets serious. "I'm sorry about all that stuff I said about you and your mom. I guess I was just worried about you, that's all. You've been so stressed out and it doesn't seem fair."

"I'm fine!" I say, but I can tell she doesn't believe me. "Okay, you're right. It's been kind of a rough few days. But I just have to be perfect from now on, that's all."

If the captain wants me to follow the rules and do everything perfectly, fine. I'll be so disgustingly perfect, he won't have any reason to single me out. Then I'll get my camera back, and Mom's job (and mine) will be totally secure.

Katy rolls her eyes. "Oh, only perfect. That sounds easy." Then she puts her arm around me. "Come on. Let's get you to the photo booth before Curt has a fit."

I'm so focused on everything going perfectly that I sail through the rest of the day. I barely pay attention to what I'm doing when I'm helping Mitch!, and my dining hall duty flies by in a mashed potato haze. By the time I get to the theater that evening, I'm barely nervous about going out onstage. Until I'm standing in the wings, that is, and then the same old room-spinning panic sets in. Thankfully, Ian materializes next to me yet again. As he escorts me out onto the stage, he whispers into my ear, "Break a leg." And that's it. I'm on the mattress, eyes closed, still breathing, and still totally awake. Maybe this perfect thing really can happen.

In the morning, I pore over the towel-folding book while Katy takes a shower. After practicing a few shapes on my own towel, I finally decide to have the class make dogs. Even though the dog instructions look a little tough, I think the kids will like it. If need be, I'll fold *myself* into a dog shape to make them happy.

"I've decided today is the day," Katy says, coming out of the teeny bathroom. Even though she doesn't have her fish tail on, she's shuffling around as if her legs are bound together. I hope she can still walk at the end of the summer. "I'm going to finally get Smith to ask me out."

"How are you going to do that?"

She sighs. "I don't know!" Then she gives me a wide smile. "Sooo, what about you? Any luck with Neil?"

I groan. "I've barely seen him. And every time I think he might ask me out, we get interrupted."

"So maybe today is the day *you* ask *him* out," Katy says.

"Are you crazy? What if he says no?"

She laughs. "Why would he?"

That's easy for her to say. She's got more confidence than five of me put together. I wish her luck—she's going to need it if she plans to have an actual conversation with Smith—and then head to my class.

As I weave through throngs of people, the ship feels jam-packed all over again. Since we're spending the day at sea, everyone is already staked out on beach chairs, ready for a day of sunbathing. I guess they've never heard about the dangers of spending so much time in the sun. Some of them are starting to look a lot like my dad's old leather briefcase.

My dad. I picture him in his small apartment, typing away on his computer while sipping his hundredth cup of tea and putting yet another pair of socks on his perpetually cold feet even though it's summer. And even though I'm still mad at him, for a second, I really miss him. He'd know what to call the teen lounge to get people to go there. He'd probably come up with a name straight out of some poem, and it would be perfect. But even if I wanted to ask him for help, I can't exactly call him from the middle of the ocean.

I shake thoughts of my dad out of my head and go inside the Fairy Fun Zone, determined to make some amazing towel dogs. The minute the kids see me, they start swarming around. There are way more of them today than yesterday since everyone's back on the ship again.

"Can we make griffins?" Nathan asks. "You know, half-lion, half-eagle creatures?"

"Towels are so boring," Jorman chimes in. "Can we pretend to be centaurs? We could fight each other!"

"No, we can be unicorns!" Sophia says. "Flying unicorns!"

"A flying unicorn is called a Pegasus," Nathan informs her.

"Peanut butter!" another boy is yelling for some reason. "Peanut butter! Peanut butter!"

"We're making towel dogs today," I announce.

"Dogs?" Jorman says, wrinkling his nose. "What's magical about dogs?"

"They're . . . a man's best friend," I say. "That's pretty magical, isn't it? They obey our commands almost like they can read our minds." The kids give me skeptical looks.

"What about fairies?" Sophia says. "Can we throw glitter and be fairies?"

"I'm a werewolf!" Jorman yells. "Awoooooooo!"

The other kids join in, and soon the entire room is howling and running around. If the captain hears us, I'm dead. I try to shush them, but that only makes the kids howl louder.

"Stop it!" I finally cry. "Stop, all of you! We're making towel dogs today and that's final! Now everyone be quiet and get in a circle!"

The enormous towel-folding book slips out of my hands and lands on the floor with a thunderous clap. All the kids jump. Then they stare at me, stunned. I realize it's the first time I've yelled at them. I feel terrible, but I have to keep this class on track.

The kids obey me without uttering a word. Sophia looks ready to cry.

"It'll be fun. I promise," I tell her, but she won't look at me. Instead, she goes to sit with Nathan as if he'll protect her from their scary teacher. Sigh.

When the kids are all in a circle, I start showing them how to make the dogs, and for once I even get it right on the first try. I proudly hold up my towel dog for the kids to see. "Now it's your turn," I tell them.

The kids barely say anything as they start working. The laughing group from the past few days is gone. I wish I could explain to them how important it is for us to follow the rules, to do everything by the book, but I don't even know if they'd listen to me.

Finally, after Nathan's gone around and inspected everyone's dog for accuracy, the class is over. The kids sit around quietly playing with their towels or having whispered conversations, clearly afraid I'm going to yell again or start throwing my giant book at them.

When Sophia's mom comes in, her forehead wrinkles. "So quiet in here today," she says. "What happened?"

I hold my breath, afraid Sophia will tell her about how I almost made her cry. But the girl simply holds out her dog and says, "Look what I made, Mommy." I could hug her.

The other kids also show off their dogs to their parents, and I can tell they're proud to have made something that looks good. But it kills me that they didn't have fun. Not even close.

Chapter 20

When I get to Blended with Love to run lines with Ian, I find him hunched over his script, mouthing words to himself.

"Sorry, I can't stay long," I tell him. "My mom needs my help with something."

"That's okay. Thanks for doing this," he says, giving me a bright smile. "I've been running the new scene all morning, so this shouldn't take long."

"I think you practice more than anyone else on this ship," I say, actually kind of impressed.

He shrugs. "I can't afford to mess up."

I almost laugh. Maybe he and I should start a

club. "I'm sure you'll do great. You're like perfect at everything."

"What are you talking about?" he says, giving me a skeptical look.

"You and Lady Lovely get a standing ovation every night. Plus, you're amazing with kids. And you saved Katy's life!"

"None of it is enough to impress my dad," he says.

"Then let's start practicing." I grab Ian's hand and pull him up, and for just a second, we stand there holding hands. A weird tingle travels up my arm, as if my skin is pulsing with electricity. But wait, this is Piggy Ian we're talking about! I don't like him. I like Neil!

I pull my hand away and the tingling fades. "Where do we start?"

We run through scenes from the final show, and this time there's even more dancing than before. Luckily, with Ian's lead, I manage to fudge my way through the dance without falling over.

When we take a water break, I'm surprised to see that we've already been practicing for a half hour. I really should go help my mom in the kitchen—with whatever "emergency" she sent me a message about after my class—but I'm actually reluctant to leave.

"So what's the deal with your dad?" I ask instead. "Why does he care what you're doing on this ship?" I seriously doubt my dad would care about how well my job is going.

Ian shrugs. "I thought if he could see me working at being an actor, and doing a good job at it, he'd finally realize that it's what I'm meant to be doing. He's never even seen me perform, but he's coming to the final night. I have to show him what I can do. Maybe then he'll take me seriously."

"Wait, your dad is on board?"

Ian lets out a long sigh. "I thought maybe you knew," he says. "He's the captain."

"The—the captain? You mean . . ." I gasp. "Do you mean Captain Hook?" This doesn't make sense. Ian is the captain's *son*? The one the captain mentioned in the towel-folding class yesterday?

"He prefers Captain Thomas," Ian says.

"But . . . but your last name isn't Thomas."

"I have my mom's."

My brain is spinning. That's why Ian was able to say all that stuff to the captain and not worry about having to walk the plank! That's why he can work here even though he's only thirteen.

"I don't tell a lot of people," Ian goes on. "I don't want them to treat me differently because of who my dad is, you know?"

"But you lied to me!"

"I didn't actually lie," Ian says. "Besides, I thought maybe your mom told you."

"My mom knows?" I shake my head. "I can't believe you didn't tell me. Is that why the captain gave us all another chance? Because you were the one who asked him to?"

"No. It's because I reminded him about second chances. Thanks to his accident, he's all about those." Ian sighs. "I was really little when it happened, so I don't remember much about it, but he seemed so different back then . . ."

But I don't want to hear it. Just when I was starting to think I might actually be able to trust Ian, it turns out he's as much of a pig as always.

"I have to go," I say, getting to my feet.

"But what about—?"

"I told my mom I'd help her with something in the kitchen."

Ian frowns. "Are you a professional chef?"

"No," I say with a snort. "I can barely make toast."

"Then why does your mom need your help at all?"

"She just does, okay?" I start walking away, but Ian follows me. He really can't take a hint.

"When was the last time you actually said no to something?" he asks.

"I said no to bacon with my eggs this morning."

"To something real."

"I don't have time for—"

"I'm serious, Ainsley," he says, gently grabbing my elbow. "When did you not do something that someone asked you to do?"

I don't know why I feel compelled to answer his

question, but I say, "My dad wanted me to come live with him for the summer, and I told him no."

Ian looks skeptical. "I'm just saying, maybe you need to let your mom fix her own problems. You can't be there for her all the time. What's the worst that will happen if you say no?"

But I don't answer. Instead, the anger inside me boils over. "You're one to talk. Everything you do is to impress your dad! Maybe things with my mom aren't perfect, but at least I'm not some pathetic puppy doing everything I can to make her like me!"

Ian looks as if I've just slapped him, but I push past him and rush for the door.

"Ainsley, wait!" Ian calls after me.

I pause for a second. "No," I say over my shoulder. Then I go to find my mom.

Chapter 21

When I get to the kitchen, I find my mom trying to calm down one of the chefs. He's pacing around and yelling out things in another language, his blond hair plastered to his face with sweat as he waves his hat around like a flyswatter.

"Ainsley, where have you been?" Mom says when she sees me. "Didn't you get my message that there was an emergency?"

"I'm sorry. I was—"

"Here," Mom says, shoving a pot of something into my arms. "Stir this, would you? Before it congeals."

I glance into the pot of what looks like—I sniff it. Yup, dog food. "What are we doing with this?" I don't think there are any pets on board, but at this point, nothing would surprise me. A llama could walk by in a belly dancing outfit and I probably wouldn't even blink.

"Meat-free chili."

I do blink. "For the *human* passengers?"

"The vegans are practically rioting, saying the entrees are inedible, so I had Hans whip up some soup for them."

"But . . . but this is disgusting!"

The chef lets out a howl beside me. "I knew it was bad!" he says in a thick accent.

"No, it's fine," Mom assures him. The she turns to me and whispers, "Please tell me you have a better idea. Thanks to your antics by the pool, the captain is already in a bad mood. We can't afford to mess anything else up."

I stare at her. Is she really blaming all this on me? "But I'm not a chef," I say. "And neither are you. It's not your job to do any of this stuff, and it definitely isn't mine!"

"Keep your voice down," she says.

But I can't stop. The words just keep pouring out. "And the whole reason Katy and I got into that fight at the pool was because of you. She was saying that I was the grown-up in our relationship and that you were the kid. What was I supposed to do? And *all* the stuff I've done since I got on board was to help you, so that you could keep this job and so that you could finally stay happy so that we could both be ourselves again! Stupid me. I thought I could actually have fun. But you know what, maybe everyone's right. Maybe I do need to let you fail at something for once."

Mom's mouth sags open. And then I see the tears forming in her eyes. Normally, I'd do anything to make them stop. Just like when I was a little kid and I'd shove all my peas into my mouth at once and force myself to swallow them down so that my mom wouldn't get upset.

But this time I stop myself. Because Ian was right. I've never said no to my mom. I've always done everything to make her happy, no matter what. And I'm sick of it. I'm tired of cleaning up her messes and only making more of my own in the process. And I'm tired of feeling as if every little thing I do is going to get us sent home.

And suddenly, I realize that I'm done. With all of it. I've had enough.

"You can try to save your job if you want," I tell her, "but when we get to Florida, I'm hopping on the next plane home."

Then I walk away. As I make my way to my room, Ian's voice echoes in my head. "What's the worst that will happen if you say no?"

I guess I'm about to find out.

When I get back to my room, my brain is still spinning. What will I do after we get back to Fort Lauderdale? I wish I could go stay with Alyssa or Brooke, but they won't be back from camp for a few more weeks. Which leaves only one option. Going to live with my dad.

I sigh and dig my dad's letter out of the bottom of my suitcase. Then I flop onto my bed and slowly unfold the thick paper.

He told me that he hoped "this letter sheds some light on things" when he gave it to me, but the first few lines made me so furious that I threw it aside and refused to even say good-bye to him before I left. But since I'm going to be spending the rest of the summer with him, I guess it's time to actually read it.

I start to skim through like I did last time, trying to decipher the scratchy handwriting, but then a phrase stops me: *I couldn't keep fixing your mother.* I swallow and start reading the letter, really reading.

I know you're still angry with me, Ainsley, but I couldn't keep fixing your mother. She wanted more and more until I had nothing left, until my life wasn't mine anymore. We both love her very much, and I understand why you would choose to live with her, but I hope you know that I wasn't abandoning you when I moved out. I was trying to stop a cycle that would only make things worse for our family. I'm afraid, though, that I see your mother relying on you more and more in my absence. I hope you'll be stronger than I was. And I hope you know that you're always welcome here with me, no matter what.

When I'm done, my chest is ready to burst. Instead of the burning anger I felt before, this time, it's something else . . . something like understanding.

All this time, I was angry at my dad for leaving us, for making my mom so upset, for upending our lives. But really, he did what I'm doing now. He was trying to get his life back.

And that's what I have to do. I've been so busy keeping my mom happy that I haven't gotten to take any pictures or have any fun or even have a real conversation with Neil. But that's going to change. If I'm only going to be on this ship for two more days, I'm finally going to say yes to what I want.

I find Neil scraping gum off a stack of recliners on the upper deck.

"Hey," I say, marching over to him, determination pumping through my veins. "How's it going?"

"Oh, you know," he says. "More grunt work."

I laugh. "I can relate."

"Really? I thought since you were Lydia's daughter, you'd get your pick of jobs."

"Nope. I get to fill in for whoever needs something." And do a million things that I know nothing about, like fixing laundry messes and figuring out vegan entrees. But not for much longer!

"But if you asked your mom to put you on a different job, she'd do it, right?"

I shrug, not wanting to get into the whole weirdness between my mom and me. "Any good vocabulary words today?" I ask, desperate to change the subject.

Neil grimaces. "I gave up. Learning words is not my thing."

"Yeah, not fun to have to study over summer vacation," I say, trying to be sympathetic.

"Did you hear the captain wants us to start learning about all the fairy tale characters on this ship so we know stuff about them if people ask?" He rolls his eyes. "I don't want to read fairy tales. Those things are for little girls."

He sounds so much like Jorman, I almost laugh. "Not all of them," I say. "In the Grimms' version of *Snow White*, the evil queen dances until she dies at the end. Not exactly little kid stuff."

But Neil doesn't seem to be listening. Instead, he glances around as if to make sure we're alone and says, "So listen, any chance you could do me a favor?"

My breath freezes in my throat. "A favor?"

"Yeah, I was hoping you could talk to your mom for me, see if she could get me a better job. Maybe working at the casino or something. I mean, being a dwarf is okay, but I'm really sick of picking up trash and stuff. And they asked me to do finger painting with kids next week." He groans. "I know you do stuff with kids, but that's really not my thing."

I take a step back. "You did see me that day at the activity center," I say. "When the kids were crawling all over me, and I was desperate for help, I thought you just didn't see me and that's why you didn't stop. But you did see me, and you just kept going."

He shrugs. "I'm terrible with kids. So anyway, will

you help me?" He flashes his adorable smile. "Please? I'd super owe you."

"I don't know," I say slowly.

"If I had a different job, I'd have more time to hang out. You know . . . with you," he says.

Oh my gosh! Is he saying he really does like me? For a second, I actually see stars. Neil likes me!!!

But then reality starts to sink in.

"Wait," I say. "Are you only being nice to me because you want my mom to give you a better job?"

He blinks. "What? No. Of course not." But he doesn't sound terribly convincing.

"Um, sorry," I say. "I, uh, have to go."

"Wait, so you're not going to help me?" he says.

"I wish I could, but . . ."

He groans. "There's no winning on this ship! I thought reporting you would get me some bonus points, but no one even cared."

"Wait. Reporting me?" I suck in a breath. It wasn't Ian who turned me in for using my camera. It was Neil! How could I have been so stupid? All this time,

I thought he might actually like me, but he was just using me. "You were trying to get me fired?"

"You're the cruise director's daughter. They're not going to fire you," he says with a shrug.

"I—I have to go," I say, and I stumble blindly away.

After my disastrous conversation with Neil, I wander around the ship for what feels like hours. I know I have to go get ready for tonight's show, but I can't seem to stop moving.

Finally, I wind up on the walking track, and I realize I'm standing where I was on that first day when I took the picture of the knitting mural. It's completely covered up now, but I can still picture it in my mind. Was the ship such a mess when it was a knitting cruise? I guess the captain would know since he used to work here back then, at least according to Adelina.

Something clicks in my brain, as if a picture is coming into focus.

Wait. Adelina didn't say he *worked* on the cruise before. She said he was here with the knitters. Does that mean . . . ?

And suddenly, I know why the man's face in the mural looked so familiar. Subtract a few years and a graying beard and a hook hand—and it's Captain Thomas! *He* used to be one of the most important knitters in the world?

The thought is so ridiculous that I laugh. It can't be true, can it? But then I remember the look of surprise on the captain's face when he was looking at the pictures on my camera. I thought he'd seen the ones I'd taken for Alyssa, but maybe it was because of the one I took of the mural. He thought his past had been all covered up, but there was a reminder staring him in the face. I wonder what Ian would say if he found out.

Ian. I shake my head and start walking again. I can't think about Ian right now.

As I pass by Blended with Love, the first thing I see is a couple smooching. Gross. But they look happy and they're holding smoothies, so that's a good sign. Then I realize that the place is full of couples. All holding hands and canoodling. Maybe the paper hearts all over the place actually helped.

"What's going on in here?" I ask Matthieu.

"I am not sure. They keep asking for some kind of license, but I don't know what they are talking about!"

I spot the old couple from the other day, the folks who were complaining about the heat, and ask them what they're waiting for.

"We're renewing our wedding vows today," the old woman says with a denture-filled smile.

"Here?"

"Yes, at the wedding chapel. I didn't realize the ship had one until that Australian fellow announced it this morning and said it was the place to go for true love."

I glance around at the other couples. Is that why they're all here? They think they're getting married?

At that moment, the door bursts open and Nathan's sister, Edwina, waltzes in with none other than Smith in tow.

"Come on!" she says to him. "Hurry up!"

Meanwhile, Smith looks completely terrified of her. "Hold on a second. I never said—"

"Yes, you did! You said I was cute. And I think you're the hottest guy I've ever seen, like something out of a fairy tale! So we're going to get married and live happily ever after!"

Smith looks around, clearly desperate, and spots me across the room. "Ashley!" he cries, rushing over to me. "Ashley, help me! That girl's crazy! She sent her mom on some made-up errand and then she dragged me here and said I have to marry her."

"Did you think about just saying no?" Yes, it's pretty ironic, me telling someone to say no, but come on!

"Smith!" Edwina calls, coming after him. "Where are you going?"

His eyes widen in panic. "She said if I refuse, she'll scream and say I was trying to kidnap her."

What a lovely girl. I'm tempted to laugh and walk away, leave Smith to deal with the mess on his own.

But I guess this is somewhat my fault since I set him up on this weird date to begin with.

"Well, the first thing we should do is find her mom," I say, but then the door swings open, and Edwina's mother runs in.

The instant she sees Smith with Edwina, she starts screaming, "My daughter! He took my daughter!"

Smith and I shake our heads wildly. No kidnapping! Promise!

"Mom, relax!" Edwina says. "We're getting married. We're in love!"

Her mom looks as if she might faint. "What are you talking about? You're just a child. You can't get married."

"Ugh," Edwina says. "Why do you have to ruin everything?"

Her mother's mouth sags open, and then a look of determination sweeps over her face. "Edwina, this is the last straw. Your father kept telling me we were spoiling you, and I finally see he was right. Now leave that young man alone and come here."

"But, Mooom!"

"Now," she says. Then she takes Edwina by the arm and drags her out of the room. As they leave, I hear Edwina's mom say, "I should have listened to your brother and taken us to that dinosaur park instead."

I barely have time to process what just happened because at that moment Mitch! comes running over to me, his face dripping with sweat as if he's been sprinting all around the ship.

"The pictures!" he says, panting. "The pictures I've been taking, they're all blurry!"

"What are you talking about?"

Mitch! shows me a bunch of photo proofs. Every single one is grainy and pixelated.

"Did you do anything to the camera when you were using it the other day?" he asks.

"No!" I say. "I was just shooting the family with the swords, and then we did the other ones, and everything was fine. I switched out the background so they wouldn't clash with it, but that was it." And then I remember. "Except . . . Oh no!" I explain to him that

I changed the photo quality so the memory card wouldn't run out of room and then forgot to tell him about it. "I'm so sorry! I didn't realize it would make them blurry!"

"It's fine," Mitch! says, but I can tell it isn't. He works on commission, so the more pictures he sells, the more money he earns. And if he sells none, then he gets nothing for all the work he's put in. And if that happens, it's all my fault.

"I'll fix this," I tell him. "Somehow I'll fix it."

Chapter 22

At the show that night, I'm a complete zombie. I barely even notice that I'm onstage. As I lie there, pretending to be asleep, all I can think about is what a mess I made out of everything. With my mom and Smith and Mitch! This was supposed to be a fresh start at sea, and instead it feels like an even bigger mess than back home.

And it doesn't help that every time I glance at Ian, a mess of emotions starts bubbling in my stomach.

After the show, since I don't have to go help my mom with anything for once, I go hang out with Katy and the other mermaids at Blended with Love.

"I'm so glad you finally came out with us!" Katy says. "We're going to have so much fun! You look great, by the way!"

I self-consciously touch my face, which feels cemented with makeup thanks to Katy attacking me before we left our room. The girl is a fairy godmother with a hot curling iron—hard to say no to. Between the makeup and the curls she insisted on, I might as well be wearing a costume.

The club is pretty much as deserted as it's always been. Once people figured out it wasn't a wedding chapel, they abandoned it. There was nothing else to keep them here. No wonder this place is always empty. Wanda the Spy is right: No matter how great the smoothies are, the atmosphere is terrible. Changing the name just confused people, as did all my little attempts to make my mom's ideas work. Well, it doesn't matter anyway, because after tomorrow, I'll be gone.

I try to have fun as Katy gossips about things going on around the ship, and Mai and Elaine giggle and smile at all the right places, but I'm too distracted to join in the conversation. Funny how annoyed I was that helping Mom kept me from having fun with kids my own age, and now that I can actually be out having fun, I can't stop thinking about the problems Mom will be dealing with when I'm no longer around.

"So what's going on with you and Smith?" I finally ask.

Katy sighs. "I still get so nervous around him! Maybe I should give up. I mean, there are plenty of other cute guys on this ship." She glances toward Curt the Spy, who's standing in the corner, looking like a secret service agent as usual.

But when he glances at Katy, I'm shocked to see his usual uptight expression totally change. He actually smiles, and I realize that Katy's right. He is cute. I was just so focused on all the bad stuff about him that I didn't see any of the good.

"What would make you come to hang out here more?" I ask her.

Katy giggles. "Cute boys."

"How about you?" I ask, turning to the other girls.

They seem stunned to actually have a chance to talk. Elaine thinks my question over for a second. "I always like free food," she says with a soft giggle.

"All the food here is free," I point out.

"Yes, but it takes too long."

She's right about that. Matthieu might be great at whipping up creations, but he needs to speed it up somehow.

"I like picture boxes," Mai says.

"Picture boxes?" I ask.

She smiles, trying to find the right words in English. "You know, the box where you take pictures with you and friends? And you make silly faces and wear hats?"

"Oh, a photo booth!" I cry.

"Yes, a photo booth!"

And then, for some reason, a snippet of one of my dad's poems pops into my head.

Is the idea the point or is the point the idea?

If you prod with it, does it leave a mark?

I never really understood the lines before, but now I wonder if my dad was saying that the whole point of coming up with ideas is to leave your mark.

Well, I'm certainly going to leave my mark on this cruise ship before I go. And this time, the idea I'm saying yes to is all mine.

I find Mom surrounded by paperwork at her desk. Her hair is a mess and her shirt seems lopsided somehow.

"Ains, come on in." Her voice is strained, as if she's worried I might start yelling at her again. But that's not why I'm here.

"I want you to let me take over the teen nightclub," I say.

"We've talked about this—"

"No, *you* talked about it, and I listened and agreed with you because I was afraid of saying no to your ideas, of making you upset. But doing that didn't help anything. I want to actually help you now. I have a great idea for the club, and I want you to let me do it."

Mom blinks, clearly surprised to hear me talking like this. "I know I depend on you too much," she says. "I thought the club was finally something I could handle on my own."

"But you can't," I say. "Let me do it, Mom. I know I can help."

She nods slowly, and I can tell I've won. "We have a lot to talk about, don't we?" she says softly.

"Yeah, I guess we do," I say. But I don't have time for that now. And honestly, I'm not sure I'm ready for it yet.

Chapter 23

The final towel-folding class is surprisingly quiet, which is good since I was up late last night figuring things out for the club. I thought the kids would be jumping for joy about the fact that they won't have to deal with me every morning anymore, but instead, Sophia comes over and wraps herself around my leg. (Thankfully, my ankle stays dry this time.)

"Can I pick stuff from the book again?" Nathan asks.

"Yes," I tell him. "But this time, we'll all be making different towel animals."

"Like what?" Jorman asks.

"Anything you want! And, if you're okay with it,

I'll display them around the ship so that other people can see them."

"Really?" Nathan says, clearly excited to show other people how amazing his work is.

"Yup."

"But shouldn't they be fairy tale-themed?" Jorman says. "It wouldn't make sense if we made trucks or something."

I bite back a smile remembering how Jorman asked if we could make exactly that on the first day. "You're right. They should be fairy tale things. So how about you go through the book and find ones you think would work?"

Jorman nods and grabs a stack of towels. He doesn't even seem to notice that they're pink anymore.

I grab some towels too, sit on the floor, and start making a dragon.

"You're doing that wrong," Nathan points out, plopping down next to me. "Do you want some help?"

My first instinct is to say no. I can figure it out on my own. But then I realize that that's what got me into trouble over and over this week. I've been agreeing to help everyone else and rejecting help when anyone offered. The only person who saw through me was Ian. Maybe that's a special pig talent or something.

"Sure," I say, scooting over so Nathan can reach the towels. "How's your sister doing?"

"She keeps complaining about how my mom is glued to her side all the time, but Mom says she's going to be grounded for weeks when we get home." He grins. "That means she won't be able to go to my birthday party."

"At the dinosaur place you were telling me about?" I say.

He nods, clearly excited. "And after that, my dad said we can get an ice-cream cake. We never have ice cream because Edwina's allergic, but he said it's my birthday, and I can have what I want."

"That's great!" I say. I still feel a little bad that I was the one who set up Edwina with Smith and caused the whole mess, but it sounds as if Edwina's spoiled brat ways would have caught up with her sooner or later. At least this way, Nathan gets to actually have some fun for his birthday.

When it's time to say good-bye, the kids huddle around and give me a huge group hug. "Make sure to stop by the teen lounge this afternoon and check out your towel sculptures," I tell them. "And if you have older brothers and sisters, tell them to come by tonight. It's going to be a great time."

"What's the lounge called?" Jorman asks.

I smile. "It's called Mirror," I say.

Mirror is full of people before I'm even done setting up. A lot of them were drawn in by the free smoothie samples outside, handed out by the evil queen from *Snow White*—er, *Schneewittchen*—i.e. one of Katy's mermaid friends with a few costume alterations. Instead of having Matthieu make smoothies one at a time, I asked him to whip up a huge batch of small samples that we could pass out. Now he's working on a few more batches so that people won't have to wait for their amazing drinks anymore.

Katy's gauzy scarves brighten up the place, and the mirrors I've hung on the walls (courtesy of Adelina) help give it some atmosphere. And the cute towel sculptures around the room add a little humor. Wanda will be happy to see that there's even a shark one.

I also made sure to put a suit of armor on Curt so that he looks like a knight from a fairy tale, and no one can see him judging and glaring. He was actually really nice about letting me dress him up.

"Should we tell everyone the booth is open?" Mitch! asks, coming over to me. "There are folks waiting already."

This is the best part of my plan. We've set up a photo station in the club where people can put on sparkly wigs and witch hats and other fairy tale-themed accessories, and then have candid pictures taken. Fun things that kids my age will actually enjoy, instead of the stiff family portraits. There's no way they won't buy prints to take home as keepsakes, which will hopefully make up for all those photos Mitch! didn't sell because of me.

"Go for it!" I tell Mitch! "Let's officially get this party started."

He gives me a big thumbs-up, looking so excited that the exclamation point after his name finally makes sense.

I hurry over to turn up the music. No more cheesy show tunes. In fact, there's nothing fairy-tale-ish about the songs I've picked; they're just a bunch of popular tunes. The captain might have a fit if he finds out, but since I won't be working here after tomorrow, it doesn't matter, right?

Someone taps me on the shoulder. I expect it to be Mitch! again, but it's Katy.

"Thank goodness I found you!" she says. "We need your help!"

I shake my head. "No way. I'm not doing any more favors for my mom." I'm surprised Mom would even bother sending Katy to find me since I thought I made it pretty clear that I was done helping her.

"No, it's not your mom who needs the help. It's Ian!"

"Ian? What happened?"

"The girl playing Lady Lovely lost her voice and can't do the show tonight. Ian said you're the only one who can take her place."

"Me?"

"You rehearsed the dance with him, right?"

"Yeah, but there's no way I'm getting onstage in front of hundreds of people and dancing! I'm not sure I can even handle waving at the crowd tonight." Let alone kissing Smith onstage, which I've totally been trying to block out of my thoughts! "Besides, how can I play Lady Lovely when I already have a part in the play?"

"I'll take over for you," Katy says. "If I put on your dress and your wig, no one in the audience will know the difference." Her eyes are gleaming with excitement. This is her chance to finally be onstage. "Come on, Ainsley. The show needs your help. It's the final night. It has to go well!"

"I wish I could help, but . . ." I don't know how to explain. I know it sounds awful to say that I'm done doing favors for people. But if I do this one, what's to stop me from doing a hundred more? No, it's time to be firm for once. If the show crashes and burns, Mom will have to deal with the consequences because that's her job. It's not mine. Not anymore. Really, it never was.

Katy sighs. "I guess that's why Ian didn't want me to ask you. He said you'd say no."

"Wait, Ian didn't send you here?"

"No. But when we found out Faria lost her voice, Ian said you were the only other person who might know the role well enough to take her place. I figured if he wasn't going to ask you then I would. Otherwise, they're going to cut his scene out of the show even though it's the most popular one!"

And that's when I realize I have to help Ian. Because this is his chance to finally prove to his dad that he belongs on the stage. If Ian doesn't do the show tonight, Captain Thomas won't get to see how amazing he is. Maybe things with my mom are too messed up to fix, but that doesn't mean Ian can't have another chance with his dad.

"You know what?" I say to Katy. "You're right. I'll do it."

Everyone is running around backstage, rushing to get ready for the show. Before I know it, someone's shoving me into Lady Lovely's dress and putting a mound of curly hair on my head.

Meanwhile, Katy is getting into my costume. She keeps shooting Smith looks across the room, and I can tell she doesn't hate the fact that she's going to kiss him. That, at least, is a serious plus of switching parts. The serious minus is having to talk and dance onstage! I start to hyperventilate just thinking about it.

"Hey, breathe," someone says in my ear. "You'll be fine."

When I turn, I'm looking right into Ian's eyes. And somehow, seeing him grinning back at me makes me a touch less petrified. It also makes me realize that I'm not even mad at him anymore. How can I be? He didn't tell people that the captain is his father because he didn't want them to treat him differently. After finding out that Neil was kissing up to me only because of my mom, I can't say I blame Ian. And all the stuff he said about my mom and about me . . . Well, it was true, wasn't it? Whether I wanted to hear it or not.

"Thanks for doing this," Ian says. "You don't have to, you know. That's why I didn't ask, because I was afraid you'd say yes even though you didn't want to do it."

I look at him. "Really?" That makes him pretty much the only person on board this ship who hasn't asked me for a favor.

"I didn't want to force you into it."

"You're not," I tell him. "I might not be great at saying no, but I'm working on it. And . . ." I swallow. "And I don't mind doing you a favor. In fact . . . I want to."

He doesn't say anything for a long minute. Then he reaches out and gently takes my hand for a second, and the energy I felt before thrums through me again.

"We're on in a minute. Are you ready?"

Even though I want to scream that I'll *never* be ready, I find myself nodding. "Are *you* ready?" I ask, realizing he looks just as nervous as I feel.

"My dad's never seen me perform before. What if he's still not convinced? I know he hates the arts, but if I can't do this anymore, I'll die. I'll turn into a total robot like he is."

Something clicks in my head. "He used to be an artist too. It was taken away from him."

Ian frowns. "What are you talking about?"

"You didn't know about his knitting?"

Ian looks at me as if I'm insane. I quickly tell him about the mural and about the picture I took. "Ask Adelina," I say. "I bet she can tell you all about it."

"But my dad hates that kind of stuff. He thinks anything 'artsy craftsy' is a waste of time."

"Maybe he does now because he can't do it anymore. But when I get my camera back, I'll show you the picture of the mural. He looked so happy." I shake my head. "The boating accident might have made him more strict, but I think not being able to do what he loves really changed him."

Ian looks stunned. "I can't believe it. But if that's true then maybe I *will* be able to convince him."

Then the music starts, the curtain opens, and it's time. Ian puts his pig head on and holds out his arm to escort me onstage. My entire body starts to freeze up, and my breath gets shallow and painful in my chest, but I force myself to take one gulp of air after another, and before I know it, Ian and I are in front of the audience. If I just look at his face and try to forget that anyone else is there, maybe I'll be okay.

Ian gives a low bow, and I manage something like a curtsy. Then he gets into waltzing position, and we start to dance. As we swish around the stage, Ian's character talks about how he was transformed into a pig. I pretend to look really interested in what he's saying, but instead, I'm scrambling to remember my lines.

There's a pause, and I realize it's my turn to speak. "How can one undo the curse?" I say, hoping my voice is loud enough.

Ian goes on to explain that he doesn't want to undo the curse. "This is who I am. Can you love me even though I am a pig?"

I look into his piggy eyes, and I realize they're not nearly as terrifying as they were that first day. "Yes," I say. "Yes, I can."

Then Ian twirls me around and around until I'm dizzy, and when we stop spinning, his mask is gone and it's just him looking back at me, smiling. And in that moment, he doesn't look like a beast at all.

Before I know it, I'm leaning in and kissing him! Even though it's not in the script at all! His lips are warm and soft, nothing like Smith's.

Then the music ends, and the audience erupts with applause. I pull away, realizing that we're still in front of hundreds of people. I'd almost forgotten. They're not giving us a standing ovation like they did when Faria was dancing, but they're not booing like I was afraid they would. And even if they were, I'm not sure I'd care, not when I can still feel the warmth from Ian's lips on mine.

Ian takes my hand, and together we rush off the stage. I'm breathing so hard, I can barely catch my breath.

As the next scene starts, Ian pulls me farther into the wings. "You were amazing," he says.

I don't know if he means the dancing or the kiss, but all I can say is, "You were too." And we stay like that, holding hands in the wings, until the end of the show. We watch the dwarves prancing and dancing—Neil still looks graceful, but I can't help noticing how bony his knees look in his tights. Why did I ever think he was the hottest guy on the ship? And at the end, when it comes time for Smith to kiss Katy, I almost burst out laughing when I see Katy cringe as his lips mash against hers. Hopefully, no one in the audience can see.

Then Katy "awakens" and sits up and gives the biggest, grandest wave imaginable. The audience cheers.

At the end, as we all go out onstage for a final bow, Mom comes out with a microphone. I suck in a breath. She still looks stressed and rumpled, and yet she's smiling. Really smiling. And her nostrils aren't twitching. She looks exhausted but happy.

She starts thanking everyone for coming and for being so great all week long, and then she starts to thank some of the people in the crew. Finally, she turns to me and says, "And biggest thanks to my daughter, Ainsley. I used to say she was my rock, but now I think she's my anchor. She grounds me when I need it, but I'm learning how to float at sea on my own without her." She gives me a tearful smile and then turns the mic over to Aussie Andy, who's ready to liven things up again.

Backstage, my mom pulls me into a long hug. "I'm sorry," she whispers into my hair. "For everything." And this time, I'm ready to forgive her.

"Come on," I tell her. "I have something to show you."

Chapter 24

When we get to Mirror, it's packed. Kids are sipping smoothies, dancing to the music, and having tons and tons of pictures taken. Mitch! is beaming with happiness, and every once in a while I see him and Matthieu exchange flirtatious smiles across the room. I can't help smiling too. Seriously, just get a bunch of people in the middle of the ocean and watch the sparks fly!

"You did all this?" Mom says. "It looks amazing."

"I had a lot of help," I tell her. For the first time in what feels like forever, I actually asked other people for help instead of being the one doing all the rescuing.

Mom goes to wander around the club to take it all in while I stand back and watch people having a great time. My heart actually swells when a girl puts a crown on her head and says, "Look, I'm Cinderella!" and a guy shakes his head and replies, "Don't you mean Aschenputtel?"

"Ainsley!" I hear Katy call as she rushes over to me, still wearing her Briar Rose costume. "Oh my gosh, you were right about Smith! Ugh, I felt like I was kissing a jellyfish! But you and Ian!" She squeals. "I can't believe it!"

I smile and shrug. "I know, but . . . I'm leaving tomorrow, so I don't know if anything will come of it."

Katy throws her arms around me. "I can't believe you're leaving. You'll always be my best cruise friend!"

I laugh. "And you'll always be mine."

She hurries off to find her other mermaid friends, and I'm surprised at how much I already miss her and her infectious giggling.

Mom comes back over and puts her arm around me. "I meant what I said earlier," she says. "When you're gone, I'll probably be a mess without you for a little while, but it's about time I stood on my own two feet. I didn't used to be like this, you know. Before you were born, I was so independent. But after I met your father, I guess I got so used to always having someone else's opinions, someone else's help, that I forgot how to do things on my own."

And maybe that's why I started doing everything on my own, I realize. So I wouldn't be like her.

"You'll be great," I tell Mom, and I mean it. Yes, her clothes might be wrinkled and her hair might be a mess, but she looks so proud of herself, so confident. I haven't seen her like that in a long, long time. I wish I could stick around longer so I'd get to see more of it.

And then it hits me. I want to stay. Yes, it's been a tough and crazy week, but I'm not ready for this adventure to be over. Not when it's only starting.

"Yes, come in," the captain says when I knock on his door a few minutes later. He doesn't look surprised to see me. "Oh, Ainsley Parker. You've come for your camera."

"Um, yeah," I say. And to ask for my job back, but that suddenly seems a lot harder than I thought it would be.

As he opens his desk, I glance at the aquarium, where the octopus is eyeing me with a strange expression on its face, almost as if it's laughing. I decide to pretend it's laughing *with* me.

When the captain goes to hand the camera over, he pauses. "I've been hearing your name come up a lot the past couple of days," he says.

I swallow. Is he going to refuse to give me my camera back because of all the stuff I messed up? That can't be legal, but he'll probably say it's his right to keep it under Sea Law or something.

"It appears I have you to thank for a lot of our successes," he goes on.

"Um, what?"

"Mirror seems to be having quite a night," he says. "Catchy name, by the way. And passengers have been buying more photos than we predicted. Not to mention your performance with my son in the show. You two make quite the pair."

I blush. "He's . . . he's a really good dancer."

"Yes, he is, isn't he? He and I had a chat after the show, and it turns out he knew things about my past that I don't normally share." He purses his lips. "But perhaps some things aren't meant to be hidden away. Anyway, we're sorry to see you go. Your mother said your mind is made up, so we wish you the best of luck."

With that, he passes me my camera. The minute it's back in my hands, I feel whole again. I'd start snapping pictures right away if I didn't think the captain would immediately toss me overboard.

He goes back to rifling through some papers on his desk, and I guess I'm dismissed. But I don't move.

"Captain? Sir?" I say. "What if . . . what if I want to stay?"

He gives me a sharp look. "Stay?"

"It's just that . . . this has been the hardest week of my life, but it's also been one of the best. I want to give it another shot. I want to stay for the summer. If you'll let me."

The captain seems to think this over a second. "It would be a shame to lose such a spirited employee," he says finally. "As far as I'm concerned, you're free to stay until the end of your contract." He clears his throat. "Provided we don't have any more mishaps, that is."

"Thank you!" I say. "Only . . . can I go ashore for a little while tomorrow before we leave port again? I need to send my dad a letter."

Captain Thomas nods. "But then get right back to work."

"Aye, aye, Captain Thomas!" I say. Then I turn and rush out of his office, excited to tell my mom—and Ian—the news.

Chapter 25

I find Mom in the Once Upon a Time Theater with Stefan. Even though it's late, they're busily going over the role changes for the next trip. I stand in the doorway, not wanting to interrupt since they seem so intent.

Not surprisingly, Katy will be taking over my role since she played the part way better than I ever could have.

"It's too bad your daughter is leaving," Stefan says. "I'd keep her as Lady Lovely and move Faria to a non-speaking dance role."

Mom sighs. "Ainsley was wonderful, wasn't she? But we'll just have to make do."

I almost laugh at that. Me, dancing onstage every night? Even a couple days ago, the idea would have been ridiculous. But now when I think about getting to perform with Ian again, the fact that I'll be onstage doesn't matter. I was so worried about letting everyone down before that I let it scare me to death. But I know that no matter how badly I mess up, Ian will be there to help me. If I need it.

I clear my throat. "Actually," I say, coming forward. "If you still want me, I think I'm going to stay."

Mom jumps to her feet. "You are? Really? But what about . . . ?"

"The captain said it was okay. And . . . I think I want to do it. But only if things don't go back to the way they were, okay?"

She nods. "Absolutely. From now on, I'm handling problems on my own." She laughs. "Although I might need your advice when it comes to replacing Smith. Any idea who might be good for the part?"

"Smith? Where is he going?" I gasp. "He didn't get fired because of that whole mess with Edwina, did he?"

"No. The captain finally understood that wasn't his fault." Mom gets a strange smile on her face. "Smith's leaving us to take another job. He's been cast in an action movie."

My jaw drops open. "No! Any idea which one?"

"Nope, but we are definitely going to be the first in line to go see it!" She starts giggling, and I can't help joining her.

After a minute, I ask, "Doesn't Ian want the part of Prince Handsome?"

"I asked him," Mom says, "but he said he's been having so much fun playing the Pig King that he didn't want to switch anymore."

"In that case, I think I know who would be perfect for Smith's part." Someone who's good-looking and totally full of himself. "Neil."

"One of the dwarves? Are you sure he can act?"

"Oh yeah," I say. "He's a great actor." He certainly had me fooled.

"Okay, we'll give it a try." Mom wraps her arm around me. "So if you're really staying, don't you think you should let a certain someone know? I saw him moping around the walking track earlier."

I smile. "Yeah, you're probably right."

It doesn't take me long to find Ian. He's leaning against the railing, looking out at the dark waves. Mom's right. His shoulders look a little more stooped than usual. Can that really be because of me leaving?

"Hey!" he says when he sees me. "Shouldn't you be packing?"

"Nope. You're not rid of me yet. I'm staying for the rest of the summer."

"Whoa, really?" He looks excited for a second. Then he frowns. "You're not just doing this for your mom, are you?"

"I'm doing it for myself. I want to stay. I haven't even gotten to take any pictures of whales or anything! It won't feel like the summer is complete if I leave now."

He nods. "Yeah, I was thinking that things are already so different after a week. I mean, my dad and I are actually talking to each other again instead of arguing. I told him I want to be an actor when I'm older, and instead of being all disappointed in me like he usually is, he said that after seeing the show tonight, he thinks I can really make it." He rolls his eyes. "He did say that if I'm going to be an actor, I better be the best one on Broadway, but you know. That's him. And he said he'll even show me some of the knitting projects he worked on years ago. I guess they've been in storage all this time."

"Wow," I say.

We stand in silence for a minute, staring out at the water, breathing in the evening air. This night feels just about perfect, but I know something that will make it even better.

"How would you like to go to a party with me?" I ask. "There's a pretty great one happening at Mirror right now."

"Oh yeah, I heard about that," he says. "Apparently some awesome girl put it together."

When we get to the club, it's absolutely packed. Everyone is laughing and talking and having an amazing time. I can't believe that I helped to make this happen.

There's so much energy and movement in the room that I instinctively grab my camera from my pocket. Then I remember that I'm Not Allowed to take pictures, and I start to put it away.

"You're not on duty, you know," Ian says. "It's okay."

He's right. So I take a picture of Matthieu and Mitch! dancing, and of Katy and Curt chatting, and of my mom putting on a silly witch hat and laughing. Then I turn and snap a couple of pictures of Ian too. After all, I have to have something to show my friends back home! Brooke will probably start howling like a monkey the minute she sees him.

"So, are you ready to do this all over again?" Ian asks.

I think about doing this crazy trip week after week, all summer long. "Probably not," I admit. "But it's going to be an adventure, right?"

Ian takes my hand. "Right."

"Then, yes," I say, and I realize I'm smiling—really smiling—for the first time in a long time. "Yes, I am."

Acknowledgments

Like Ainsley, I have a hard time saying no to people, but I'm so glad I said yes to this project! Big thanks to Erin Black and the rest of the Scholastic crew for giving me a chance to set sail with Ainsley and her mom. Also, eternal thanks to my family members for all their help, to Ammi-Joan Paquette for her guidance, to Sarah Chessman for her willingness to answer strange questions, and to Tiffany Sparks-Keeney for her cruise-ship input (and to Joy McCullough for putting us in touch). Finally, thank you to Lia for being the most adorable kind of distraction, and to Ray Brierly for always being my anchor.

About the Author

Anna Staniszewski is the author of the My Very UnFairy Tale Life series, the Dirt Diary series, and the Switched at First Kiss series. She also wrote the picture book *Power Down, Little Robot*. She lives outside of Boston with her family and teaches at Simmons College. When she's not writing, Anna reads as much as she can, eats lots of chocolate, and enters "Belly Flop Like an Ogre" competitions. Visit her online at www.annastan.com.